The Bookstore on Marco Island

Scott Sisters Series — Book 1

AMY RAFFERTY

&

ROSE RYAN

THE BEACH HOTEL ON MARCO ISLAND

SCOTT SISTERS SERIES - PREQUEL

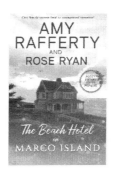

When the Scott family gathers on the beautiful Marco Island to celebrate their mother's 65th birthday, six sisters feign happiness in the face of their mother's "predictions" and their father's poor health. But each sister is followed by their own problems, causing a tangled mess of drama thinly veiled behind fake smiles.

Lorry's daughter blames her for the divorce between her parents.

Nicole is a cancer survivor grappling with being unable to conceive and her husband's reluctance to adopt.

Stephanie faces the anxiety of her husband wanting more children to add to their picture-perfect family.

Ashley and her husband struggle with IVF and the stress of managing a successful new restaurant together.

Hannah is overwhelmed with the plans for her wedding to her cardiologist fiancé, leaving her to brush off her family's poking and prodding.

Meanwhile, Jessica aches to finally set a wedding date with her fiancé Trent, who seems hesitant to commit.

In an emotionally charged tale of family, romance and womanhood, six sisters must wade through their complicated lives to save their family from crumbling.

DOWNLOAD FOR **FREE** ~ Click Here

AMY RAFFERTY VIP READERS

Don't want to miss out on my giveaways, competitions, and

'hot off the press' news?

Subscribe to my email list.

It is FREE!

Click Here!

CONNECT WITH AMY RAFFERTY

Not only can you check out the latest news and deals there, you can

also get

an email alert each time I release my next book.

Follow me on BookBub

I always love to hear from you and get your feedback.

Email me at ~ books@amyraffertyauthor.com

Follow on Amazon ~ Amy Rafferty

Sign up for my newsletter and free gift, Here

Join my 'Amy's Friends' group on Facebook

CONNECT WITH ROSE RYAN

Sign up for my newsletter and keep up on all the latest book news,

release dates,

excerpts, monthly giveaways, and more!

Or follow me on my other socials including:

Facebook , **Instagram**, **Bookbub** , and **Goodreads**

Follow my author central page on Amazon: **Rose Ryan:**

TABLE OF CONTENTS

1.	CHAPTER 1	1
2.	CHAPTER 2	15
3.	CHAPTER 3	28
4.	CHAPTER 4	46
5.	CHAPTER 5	60
6.	CHAPTER 6	79
7.	CHAPTER 7	96
8.	CHAPTER 8	114
9.	CHAPTER 9	132
10.	CHAPTER 10	147
11.	CHAPTER 11	168
12.	CHAPTER 12	184
	CONTINUE THE SERIES	202
	SCOTT SISTERS SERIES	218

ALSO FROM AMY RAFFERTY   219

COMING SOON FROM AMY RAFFERTY   222

MORE BOOKS BY AMY RAFFERTY   238

AMY RAFFERTY VIP READERS   242

CONNECT WITH AMY RAFFERTY   243

CONNECT WITH ROSE RYAN   245

A NOTE FROM AMY RAFFERTY   246

A NOTE FROM ROSE RYAN   248

CHAPTER 1

The Florida sun began its descent towards the horizon, casting hues of pink and orange across the sky, painting a beautiful but bittersweet scene outside Nicky's window. Inside, she sat in the living room of her cozy Miami home, her heart fluttering with a mix of emotions. She'd just started the adoption process, determined to fulfill her dream of becoming a mother.

Nicky looked at her wristwatch. It was almost time for her husband, Eric Rogers, to arrive home. He'd been away on another business trip for nearly fifteen days. Eric was more away on business than he was at home these days. Nicky let out a breath as nerves gripped her, and her eyes fell on the forms on the coffee table in front of her.

They were the adoption papers. Nicky had completed what she could and now needed Eric's signature. With him away so much these past few months, she'd taken the initiative to start the process on her own. She took a sip of the smooth merlot she held in a hand that shook slightly and smiled when her four-year-old basset, Belvedere, gave a low moan and adjusted his head on her lap.

"I wish I could just put my head on a warm lap and have all my troubles dissolved by someone stroking my hair." Nicky laughed as he wiggled his head, nuzzling her free hand to get more attention.

"I'm back." Eric's voice jolted her heart and elicited a head lift and bark from Belvedere.

"I'm in the living room," Nicky called. "I'm having a glass of wine. Would you like one?"

Eric walked in, loosening his tie as he stopped near where she was sitting and shook his head.

"No, thank you," Eric replied. "I think I'm going to have a shower." He sniffed the air. "What are you cooking?"

"I thought I'd make your favorite pot roast," Nicky answered.

"I wish you'd told me you were cooking," Eric said. "Then I wouldn't have stopped to grab a bite to eat on my way home."

"Oh!" Nicky's heart dropped as she saw his drawn features.

He was tired from traveling, and she knew that look. It meant he wouldn't be in the mood for heavy conversation. He would climb into bed after his shower, put the television on, and watch the news until he fell asleep.

"I'm sorry, Nicky," Eric said, blowing out a breath. "I'm exhausted."

"I can see that." Nicky gave him a tight smile.

She gently pushed Belvedere from her lap, leaned forward, and placed her wine glass on the coaster on the coffee table. Nicky picked up the adoption forms and stilled her beating heart. She knew that when he went to have his shower, he wouldn't discuss anything after that, and she wasn't going to wait another day to discuss it.

"Eric," Nicky said, holding his gaze with hers. "We have something to discuss, and I'm sorry. I know you're tired, but I'm tired of you constantly not having time to discuss the matter with me."

"Matter?" Eric's eyes narrowed as they fell on the documents she cradled to her chest as she stood. "What matters do we have to discuss?"

His six-foot frame seemed broader. Nicky's eyes traveled over his torso, noting how his shirt strained over his muscles, and she frowned.

"Have you been working out?" Nicky asked him, her frown deepening when she noticed that the gray streaks that had been forming in his hair were all gone. "And you dyed your hair?"

"Nicky, you know I have to look good for my job," Eric said impatiently. His eyes dropped to the documents once again. "What is it you want to discuss?"

His eyes narrowed to slits and were filled with suspicion as they met hers.

"I need you to sign these forms." Nicky handed them to him. "I started the adoption process this week."

"Why would you do this without consulting me?" Eric's voice turned cold, and his eyes blazed with anger. "It's not something you had the right to start behind my back. It's a decision we both needed to make and be in agreement about before starting the process."

"I've tried talking to you about it for months, Eric. You're always away, and every time I bring it up, you brush me off," Nicky responded, her voice trembling with hurt over his reaction and frustration.

"You know I'm busy with work," he retorted, his anger intensifying. "You also know how I feel about adoption!" He seethed and shoved the documents in her face. "Did you think by blindsiding me with this, it would change my mind?"

"I'd hoped that you would finally consider it now that the proceedings have been started." Nicky kept her voice level and curled her nails into the soft flesh of her palm to steady her emotions. "Filling in a few forms is not committing to anything."

"Oh really?" Eric hissed and shuffled through the papers in his hand. "As soon as you hand this document in, we start getting vetted." His eyes turned even stormier. "Next thing, our lives will be sifted through with a fine-tooth comb."

"So?" Nicky's face scrunched into a scowl. "We have nothing to hide!"

"That's not the point!" Eric raised his voice and dumped the documents on the coffee table. "You want kids so badly—" He cut his words off and glared at her. "You adopt them on your own." His hands clenched into fists. "I'm done!"

With that, Eric spun on his heel and stormed out of the room. A whine from the sofa caught Nicky's attention, and she turned to see Belvedere cowering there, her heart dropping.

"Oh, no, boy!" Nicky dropped to her knees beside him and stroked his fur soothingly. "This isn't about you, sweet boy."

Belvedere lifted his head and gave Nicky a few doggy kisses on the cheek. He soothed her rumpled emotions as much as she did his.

"Why can't relationships be this easy to soothe, huh?" Nicky stood, picked up her wine glass, and walked through to the kitchen.

She poured the remaining contents of the glass into the sink, washed her hands, and started finishing off the pot roast that she decided to put in the refrigerator to heat up the next day. Nicky finished cleaning up the kitchen, poured herself another glass of wine, and walked back into the living room with Belvedere at her heels.

She'd just sat on the sofa to watch the last rays of sun slip behind the inky night curtain when she heard Eric thumping down the stairs. Nicky frowned and was about to get up to find out what was going on when he popped into the room. His hair was still damp from the shower, and he'd changed into a pair of jeans with a cotton shirt and loafers.

Nicky frowned and looked at the two large suitcases he held in each hand with a yellow envelope shoved beneath his arm.

"Eric, what's going on?" Nicky sat forward on the sofa and put her wine on the coffee table as she looked at him questioningly. "Are you off on another business trip?" She shook her head. "You've only just gotten home."

"No." Eric shook his head, and his face was a blank slate as he left his suitcases and stepped toward her. "I'm leaving, Nicky."

"To go where?" Nicky asked, confusion swirling around her.

"To where I should've gone a while ago," Eric told her, his voice emotionless. "Every time I tried to leave, something in your life would blow up, and I couldn't leave you."

"I don't understand." Nicky's heart was pounding in her chest, and a whooshing had started in her ears.

"Maybe this will clear things up for you." Eric handed her the envelope from beneath his arm. "I had it finalized yesterday."

Nicky stared at the item he held out to her, afraid to touch it as she instinctively knew that the contents of it were about to blow up her life. She didn't know if she could step onto another landmine. When she didn't move to take the document, Eric let out a breath and dropped it on the coffee table beside the adoption papers she'd dumped there earlier.

"Is this about the adoption process?" Nicky asked him.

"No, Nicky, it's not just that." Eric let out another breath and ran his hand through his hair. "This has been a long time coming." He glanced out the large windows that overlooked the bay before turning back toward her. "Seven years, to be exact."

"Seven years?" Nicky's brows were knit into a tight frown.

Eric huffed, his shoulders squared, and his jaw tightened. "Look, there's no easy way to do or say this, so I'm just going to come straight out with it." He looked at the envelope he'd put on the table. "Those are divorce papers. I've signed everything over to you. I went to the bank and took my name off our joint account, so all the savings in there are also yours."

"Divorce?" The words felt like barbed wire being ripped out of her throat. "Because I want to adopt a child?"

"No, Nicky, this isn't just about that." Eric was getting more and more impatient. "I fell out of love with you a long time ago when I met Sophie."

"Sophie?" Nicky's head was spinning, and she felt like she was having a bad dream or one of those nightmares where you didn't realize you were having a nightmare. "Your receptionist?"

"She's a lot more than a receptionist!" Eric growled defensively. "She's also a fully trained yoga instructor."

"Right!" Nicky nodded, knowing she was being condescending, but she couldn't help it. "Because that's a whole step up from being able to manage a switchboard."

"Don't act like a jealous shrew, please," Eric breathed. "It doesn't suit you."

"Jealous?" Nicky looked at him in disbelief. "This isn't me being jealous. This is me in a state of shock!" She pushed herself to her feet and stood, looking at him as if he'd grown two heads. "Which I have every right to be." She pointed at the ground with her index finger as she spoke. "My husband of fifteen years just told me that he's leaving me for another woman he's been having an office affair with for the past seven years!"

"What Sophie and I have is much more than an office affair," Eric informed her. "I'm madly in love with her, and the reason I don't need or want to adopt is that we have a beautiful five-year-old son, and in two months, we'll have a baby girl."

His words felt like he'd punched her in the heart, cracking open their marriage and breaking apart the foundations of the life they'd made together. Nicky's heart shattered as the wrecking ball of his betrayal smashed through it, making her feel ill. Her legs felt like they would collapse at any moment as her soul trembled, shaking her core.

"I don't want a big scene over this," Eric said coldly. "I've been really fair by giving you the house, our savings, and everything, except for a few items listed in the divorce settlement."

"You think that's fair?" Nicky breathed in disbelief, her eyes widening at his words as she tried to keep her head above the swirling ocean of emotions rising inside her. "This is my house. I was the one who bought it. So, thank you for being fair and giving me *my* house!"

"Don't be like that, Nicky." Eric turned his face slightly. "There's no need for this to get ugly."

"Then I suggest you leave right now," Nicky advised. "And the words you should've said are uglier." Her lips curled in a sneer as the anger over his betrayal hit her fast and hard. "Because you made this ugly the minute you decided to cheat on our marriage. Or maybe that should've been even uglier." She advanced toward him, driven by the rage, humiliation, and hurt surging through her. "Because while you watched me suffer through miscarriage after miscarriage, you were starting a family with someone else."

"Nicky, that wasn't planned!" Eric's eyes widened, and he held his hands up in front of him, taking a step back.

"Where are you going to live?" Nicky asked as a terrible thought struck her.

"I bought another house where Sophie and Gray live." Eric eyed her warily.

"Gray?" Just when Nicky didn't think he could squeeze more blood from her bleeding heart, he did. "You named your son Gray!"

"We both chose that name, and after your first miscarriage—" Eric stopped talking and swallowed as he glanced at her clenched fists.

"You thought what?" Nicky breathed furiously. "I wasn't going to ever use the name, so you and your mistress may as well use it like a pair of cast-off shoes."

"Be fair, Nicky!" Eric warned her. "Remember, I've been very lenient with my demands for the divorce."

"Oh wow!" Nicky's voice resonated with sarcasm. "You're the one that cheated and had a secret family for seven years, but *you've* got demands," she pointed out. "I'll bet if I check on who paid for the house your second family is living in, I own half of it." She knew she was being petty, but she couldn't help it. Her mind was reeling and in a total state of confusion. At that moment, she was powered by her anger, hurt, and shock. "The car you drive." She pulled a face. "I bought that too. It's also in my name because your credit is shot because of all your bad business startups."

"There's no need to rub your success in my face, Nicky!" Eric's eyes lit with anger once again. "At least I wasn't the one that failed at the one thing we wanted most in our lives." He looked at her smugly as his words made her flinch like he'd slapped her. "Having a family."

"Get out!" Nicky said through gritted teeth. "I'll have my attorney look over the divorce papers first thing in the morning and send any amendments through, as well as any audits I may need."

"I told you I've given you everything in the divorce." Eric's eyes widened at the word audit, which sent alarm bells ringing in her head. "There's no need for audits, Nicky. Please, I just want us to have an amicable divorce."

"Oh!" Nicky's voice took on an I-understand-now tone, and she saw him look at her warily for a few seconds. "How silly of me to get upset." She relaxed her features, and she saw him visibly relax. "I'm sorry for being such a... what did you say?" She frowned as if trying to remember what he'd called her earlier. "Oh, yes, a jealous shrew." She rolled her eyes mockingly. "You know what?" She had wide eyes. "I'll see my attorney first thing in the morning, sign off on the divorce, and then we can all have Sunday lunch and be good friends."

His brow furrowed as he stared at her intently, trying to figure out if she was being serious.

"Are you being serious?" Eric asked, looking at her with uncertainty.

"NO!" Nicky fumed, her chest rising and falling as she felt her anger wanting to spew out like a fire-breathing dragon and burn him to cinders. "If you wanted an amicable divorce, you never should've cheated on me in the first place, let alone have a second secret family that I've probably been supporting while I also funded your new business."

"Nick, don't start a war over this, please," Eric warned her.

"You started it seven years ago," Nicky pointed out. "Now, please leave my house."

"I'll call you tomorrow about picking up the rest of my things." Eric had the audacity to say as he turned to get his suitcases.

"No, you won't." Nicky walked with him to the front door and held out her hand. "I want your house keys."

"How will I get back in to collect the rest of my stuff?" Eric asked her in disbelief.

"I have my people call yours." Nicky finally got to say the line she'd always wanted to say but didn't expect to say to her husband. "Keys, please, and just be thankful I'm letting you take the car."

Eric's eyes widened even more as he quickly pulled the house keys and gate remote from his key ring and handed them to her. He was halfway through the door when he stopped and turned toward her. Nicky saw a flicker of remorse flash in his eyes for the first time that evening.

"Nick..." Eric started to say, but she held her hand up, silencing him.

"Whatever you have to say, pass it on to my attorney," Nicky told him, slamming and locking the front door once he'd stepped through it.

She knew it was childish, but it felt good to slam the door in his face, and she couldn't help thinking how final it was as she closed the door on yet another chapter of her life. After which, she leaned her forehead against the front door, twisted so her back was against it, and slid to the floor. Hugging her knees to her chest, she burst into tears when a wet nose was pushed between her arms. Nicky wrapped her arms around Belvedere and sobbed into the night.

Pent-up emotions, frustrations, and stress from the past five years of her life burst like an overflowing dam as the house around her drifted into darkness. Through her oophorectomy four years ago and her father's death three years ago, just before Eric started his new business, Nicky had held herself together. But she no longer had anything to hold onto, and she'd run out of emotional duct tape as she curled into a ball next to the front door, sobbing into the soft fur of her faithful companion.

CHAPTER 2

Six months later

Nicky stood on the balcony of her Coconut Grove home overlooking Biscayne Bay. She leaned on the railing, closed her eyes, and drew a deep breath, letting her mind wander back to the day she'd found the house.

It was ten years ago, and Nicky had found out she was pregnant. She hadn't had the chance to tell Eric because, as usual, he was away on a business trip, traveling with one of the many sports stars he represented as a sports management agent. At the time, he was working for All-Star Sport Management.

Nicole swallowed as the memories played through her mind like a movie, and she watched moments of her life play out. Eric had given her the go-ahead to choose the home they were going to start a family in. The only thing he'd helped her decide on was the neighborhood, Coconut Grove.

She snorted, realizing that she'd spent most of their marriage making the decisions and was the only one who was really present in them. Nicole had been the one to find their home, set up their joint bank account, and make sure they had separate attorneys, life insurance, and medical insurance. It was Nicole who planned and organized their holidays and their lives.

Nicky shook her head, opened her eyes, and remembered seeing this view for the first time. It had taken her breath away, and she knew this house was where she wanted to raise a family. She swallowed back the tears stinging her eyes and pursed her lips. This house was meant to be filled with love, laughter, and a warm family.

Like it had before. She'd bought it from a lovely couple retiring to Tampa to be near their grown children. Children that had grown up in this house. Her eyes fell on the big tree perched on the side of the neatly manicured lawn. Nicky had pictured it with a fort in it and a playground set around it where she and Eric's children would play.

But that never happened for Nicky and Eric, and the house had always felt sad, empty, and lonely. It had been built with love by the couple who'd owned it and had been filled with a family of six. Nicky had hoped for a family of five, having grown up with five sisters in a large home filled with love and laughter.

Nicky had always felt the echoes of the family that had once lived in the house. After each tragic miscarriage, she'd come home to her house and felt it embrace her. She knew it sounded whacky, but one of the reasons Nicky managed to pick herself up after each loss was because of the energy she drew from her home—remnants of the warmth and joy that the house had absorbed from the happy family that had lived there before her.

It had broken her heart when she'd put it on the market, and she was surprised when it sold so quickly after it had been listed. Nicole had spent two weeks deciding between taking it off the market and accepting the offer. That was until she had the misfortune of running into Eric and Sophie. They were having dinner with a sports star at the same restaurant where she was having dinner with one of her authors.

Nicole had chosen to ignore them and concentrate on the author, who had just written their third international best seller. They were having dinner to celebrate and discuss his book tour. She knew it was petty, but when she saw the look on Eric's face when he saw her with the handsome and enigmatic Drew Davenport, it gave her great satisfaction. It had been even more satisfying when Eric dragged Sophie to her table to say hello. Sophie was surprised when she found out who Drew was.

The best part of that evening was introducing Eric as her ex-husband and Drew taking her hand from across the table to raise it to his lips and tell her his loss was Drew's gain. Eric had not been amused, and Sophie had gushed at how great Drew's books were. And she couldn't wait for his next novel, which had made Eric even more annoyed. Nicky smirked to herself as she remembered how Eric had stormed away after Sophie asked Drew to autograph his latest novel she had in her purse. It was also that moment that made Nicky realize it was time to go home and leave Miami behind.

"Are you ready, Nicky?" Hannah, Nicky's second-youngest sister, asked from the sliding door.

Nicky turned to look at her. "After ten years, you still won't come onto the balcony?"

"You know I don't like balconies." Hannah shuddered.

Nicky knew she was thinking about when Hannah worked for Doctors Without Borders after finishing medical school. Hannah was on a remote island that had been devastated by a tropical storm and was combing through the wreckage with the rescue crews. She found a young girl and her brother huddled on a balcony on top of a hill. The house had become unstable, and the rescue team was worried about stepping onto the balcony.

Hannah was the smallest of the crew and instantly volunteered. She managed to get to the children and got the little girl off when the balcony broke off from the main house. Hannah grabbed the little boy, shielding him as best she could as the structure slid down the hill. While the little boy had only suffered minor injuries as Hannah had protected him, she'd been trapped beneath the structure and sucked into the mud. Hannah had barely escaped the ordeal with her life and had sustained major injuries. It had been weeks of touch and go for her sister, a nightmare Nicky hoped never to relive.

Since then, Hannah didn't go out on balconies and had to force herself to walk over a back-garden deck only a few feet off the ground.

"Wouldn't you tell your patients they needed to take a few steps toward their fears and slowly walk through them?" Nicky asked.

"It depends how bad their fear is," Hannah told her. "And I have taken my first few steps toward walking through my fear." She grinned proudly and expanded her arms. "See, I'm standing in the doorway."

"Only because I ignored the first five or six times you yelled for me from the living room." Nicky laughed as Hannah's eyes narrowed.

"So, you did hear me!" Hannah huffed.

"Yes, I was having a few moments with my house." Nicky sighed and turned to take one last look at the bay. "I'm going to miss it."

"You spent the past ten years of your life here, Nicky." Hannah's voice dropped to a soothing tone. "It's always going to be a part of you now, just like your memories will echo through the halls for generations to come."

"Okay!" Nicky shook her head at her sister, who was quoting her. "Let's get going."

"Good because we're leaving two hours late, and I've already had four calls from Mom asking me when we're leaving Miami." Hannah rolled her eyes and stepped into the living room.

Nicky took one last look at the view and back garden, silently saying goodbye to her past. She turned and entered the living room, where Hannah and Belvedere were waiting for her. Hannah had come to help Nicky pack up her life in Miami, tape up the pieces of her shattered marriage, and journey to Marco Island with her into the new chapter of her life.

As they left Miami behind, Nicky felt herself relaxing, and a flicker of excitement sparked inside her. She was leaving all her heartache and stress behind her in the hustle and bustle of the big city. Nicky had thought throwing herself into her work and keeping her and Eric's lives together would help her heal from the scars of her past. But she'd been wrong. All that did was cover the wounds still festering underneath the tender facade. Nicky had known that three years ago when she'd gone to Marco Island for her mother's sixty-fifth birthday. As soon as she crossed the town border of Marco Island, Nicky felt herself start to heal.

The last few Christmases, she'd gone back to be with her family, and although they felt the loss of their father, something inside her felt like it was mending. For two months after Eric left her, Nicky wanted to get in her car and run home to Marco Island. After endless calls to her mother and sisters, Nicky finally decided it was time for a change. She'd been growing dissatisfied at work for two years, and her dream of owning a bookstore had grown stronger.

But she had to push it aside to finance Eric's business venture, Rogers Sports Management.

"You were telling me about the final divorce settlement," Hannah reminded her as she settled into the passenger seat.

Nicky glanced in the mirror to ensure Belvedere was okay in the back. He was sleeping, stretched out on the back seat.

"Oh, yes," Nicky said, recalling being interrupted by the movers. "We got busy with the movers."

"I still think you need a bigger storage space than a ten-foot lock-up," Hannah told her before moving the subject back to the divorce.

"You were about to tell me how your lawyer basically ripped up the divorce contract and started again."

"She didn't exactly rip it up," Nicky said. "She shredded it with her new shredder."

"Rebecca Dean is a tough attorney." Hannah's eyes widened, and she blew out a breath.

"Rebecca believes in fairness and said the divorce was nowhere near fair." Nicky pulled into the middle lane to get past a truck. "She said that Eric's attorney had tried to sweeten it by having Eric not contest the ownership of the house and giving up the substantial savings in the joint account."

"I can see why Rebecca would pounce on that." Hannah agreed with Rebecca's findings. "You bought the house, and the money in the joint account was all yours."

"I know, but I never saw it that way." Nicky felt small and petty again. "We were married, and as far as I was concerned, we shared everything."

"And then some!" Hannah's voice was laced with anger. "You financed his life, his business, the secret house for his *other* family, and a brand-new car for her."

"That's why Eric wanted me to accept our house and what was left of the money in our joint account." Nicky cleared her throat as pain and anger washed through her at the reminder of what the audit had found.

"It was why he balked and tried to stop you from getting your legal team to go through everything you owned." Hannah's eyes blazed as they narrowed into slits. "Gran was right. Eric had a shadow side to him that he hid from you."

"Oh, yes, Gran!" Nicky sighed. "I love her to the moon and back, but I hate it when she's always eerily right about things."

"I don't think even she saw that Eric had another family you were supporting," Hannah said. "I cannot believe that man. I'm glad your attorney took over and redid the divorce terms." She gave a smug smile. "Which he couldn't contest, and now you get most of his profits from his new business alliance with All-Star Sport Management."

"Yes, that merger was the reason he could finally get a divorce from me!" Nicky couldn't stop the bitterness and anger in her voice. "He no longer needed me to fund his life." She took a breath to calm the anger that was resurfacing and was supposed to have been left behind in Miami. "Sorry, Han, I didn't mean to get all venomous there."

"Oh, no, please!" Hannah pulled a face. "You need to get a *lot* more venomous about this than you have been." She raised her eyebrows. "That snake used you and then tried to get rid of you as soon as he suddenly came into a fortune so he wouldn't have to share it with you."

"I don't like to think that was his intention." Nicky bit her lip. No, Hannah was right. Eric was using her to fund his and his other family's life. He was the worst kind of snake.

"It most certainly was, and I'm so thankful for Rebecca Dean." Hannah shook her head. "I think she deserves a medal."

"I honestly just wanted it all over with," Nicky said honestly. "I want to move on now and start a new chapter of my life."

"Well, with the sale of your house, what was left of your savings, and the monthly revenue from your share of the All-Star Sport Management and Rogers Sport Management amalgamation. You can do so quite comfortably, too." Hannah pointed out.

"I'm thinking of investing most of it," Nicky voiced her plans. "And I want to find a nice little store to start a bookshop that has a coffee shop."

"I was just about to say that," Hannah told her. "You had a dream to start Cozy Corner Coffee and Books."

"You remember that?" Nicky smiled at her sister.

"Of course, I do," Hannah said. "Jess even drew you sketches for the store."

"Yes, and she made me samples of homemade coffee cups, plates, and even cutlery." Nicky's mind raced as her dream of owning her store resurfaced.

"Oh, gosh, yes, they were gorgeous." Hannah turned in her seat to look at Nicky. "I think Gran uses them for her special readings."

"She does." Nicky nodded. "It's going to be nice to stay at Scott House until I find a place to live."

"I'm thinking maybe a cottage near Scott House," Hannah suggested.

"Maybe." Nicky shrugged. "I'm not looking that far ahead. Right now, I'm just getting through each day one step at a time."

"Exactly!" Hannah agreed. "And there's no hurry because I know for a fact that Mom is looking forward to having you at home."

"It's just her and Gran in that big house now." Nicky glanced out the window as they drew closer to Marco Island.

"I love this part of the drive as we pull into town." Hannah rolled down her window and stuck her head out.

"Me too," Nicky admitted, slowing down as they neared the town. "I start to relax and get a warm feeling." She glanced at the blue sea. "Suddenly, you know everything's going to be all right."

"Because you're home!" Hannah turned toward her, and Nicky saw she felt the same way. "I've always felt that no matter where I move in the world, that's the new place I live, but Marco Island—this is my home."

"We were born here and are part of the island's heart," Nicky repeated something their grandmother always said.

"Nicky!" Hannah squealed, giving Nicky such a fright that she nearly swerved off the road. "Stop the car!"

"What?" Nicky's eyes widened, and she glanced around, wondering if she had ridden over something. Her heart was pounding and making a roaring noise in her ears. "What happened?"

She pulled over as soon as possible and stopped the car, feeling shaken.

"Nothing happened!" Hannah said excitedly, opening the car door and jumping out. "Come and look at this."

"Look at what?" Nicky said, confused and still shaken.

But Hannah was already out of the car and rushing toward the small block of shops at the end of Tigertail Avenue, the road where Scott House and Scott Hotel were.

"Nicky!" Hannah shouted, and Nicky could see her beckoning to her as she glanced in the mirror.

Taking a breath to calm her nerves, Nicky looked at Belvedere.

"Do you need to stretch your legs?" she asked him and got a small woof in response.

Nicky quickly put his leash on his harness and let him out of the car as she walked over to Hannah, who was practically bouncing with excitement.

"What has got you jumping up and down like a kid with too much sugar in their system?" Nicky asked.

"Look!" Hannah grabbed Nicky by the shoulders and spun her around to look at the corner shop.

"Yes, it's Sully's Corner Book Store." Nicky pointed with her hand. "I've seen the store a million times. I used to go in there every day when I was younger."

"Look closer!" Hannah instructed.

Nicky rolled her eyes, and that's when she saw it. In fact, she didn't know how she'd missed it. Her heart stopped for a few seconds before jolting in excitement, and her eyes widened.

"It's for sale!" Nicky breathed, hardly believing her eyes and looking at her sister, dumbstruck. "It's for sale."

"Yes, it is!" Hannah nodded. "Now, if that's not kismet, I don't know what it is."

Woof, woof! Belvedere agreed with Hannah.

CHAPTER 3

Mike Sullivan stood in the quaint little bookstore, Sully's Corner, surrounded by shelves upon shelves of books. It had been his uncle Angus's sanctuary for as long as he could remember, and now, with Angus gone, it fell upon Mike to decide its fate.

Mike drew in a deep breath of the salty ocean as the soft breeze from the nearby Tigertail Beach rustled the pages of the old books while he and his childhood friend, Harry Beckett, took stock of the bookstore.

As they went through the books, Mike had to push the nagging feeling of indecision from his mind and the sense that he was letting his uncle down aside. His eyes scanned the heavy oak shelves, which still shone from the love and care Angus gave them at least four times a year.

Every season brings about change, Mike, my boy. You need to clean away the buildup from the last season so you can embrace the new one free of dust. That goes for everything in life, including this old shop.

Mike gave a soft snort as he pictured his uncle standing with his mug of steaming coffee and the double wooden glass doors wide open as he welcomed in the morning. Angus was a tall man with broad shoulders who stood up straight and proud until the day he died.

Mike shook his head as the confusion over Angus's sudden death once again swirled inside of him. The doctors weren't sure about the cause of his death but suspected a heart attack. How do you suspect someone died of a heart attack? Mike pushed the thought aside as it baffled, angered, and saddened him.

Mike was twenty-two when his parents died in a car crash. He'd spent a lot of summers on Marco Island with his uncle, and after Mike's parents died, Angus had been there for him. Just like he'd been there for Mike when Mike's younger sister, Trinity, and her husband, Brian, had died five years ago. Mike had been left as the guardian and caretaker of his nine-year-old niece, Jade.

Mike rubbed his eyes. He didn't know how he'd have coped with being a single parent if it hadn't been for Uncle Angus. Mike let his eyes drift around the store that held a lifetime of memories—memories he wasn't sure he was ready to let go of just yet but knew he had to. Keeping the store was not a practical move.

"You know, Mike, selling this place just doesn't sit right with me," Harry said, running his fingers over the spines of the books. "Angus was like a second father to me. This store was his life."

Mike sighed, feeling torn. "I know, Harry, but I can't help but think about the practical side of things. I live and work in Miami now. Jade has her life there too, and running a bookstore on Marco Island seems impossible."

"But this place meant so much to Angus," Harry persisted. "It was more than just a bookstore to him; it was his connection to this island and its people."

"I understand that, Harry," Mike replied, feeling the weight of the decision on his shoulders. "But I have to be practical. I have my own life and responsibilities in Miami."

"You keep saying that," Mike pointed out. "Which makes me wonder who you're trying to convince: me or yourself!"

"I'm not sure, my friend." Mike sighed and looked through the doors.

The bookstore fronted Tigertail Beach, which stretched its white sandy shores into the deep blue ocean, painting a tranquil picture as the backdrop for Sully's Corner.

"Remember when your sister, Trinity, and her husband, Brian, died, and you were left shell-shocked by their deaths and having to care for a nine-year-old girl?" Harry reminded him. "Angus stepped in without hesitation and offered to take Jade."

Mike nodded, feeling a lump form in his throat. "He loved Jade as if she were his own granddaughter. He was the only family we had left, and he took that role seriously."

"Yeah, I know," Harry said, a small smile forming. "Well, look at Jade now. She's grown into a fine young woman. She's smart, talented, and passionate about reading and horses, just like her great Uncle."

"Hey, I'd like to think I had something to do with that." Mike smiled at the thought of Jade, his heart swelling with pride.

"Of course, but Angus made it much easier for you," Harry said.

"She's doing so well in school." Mike jumped at the opportunity to turn the conversation away from Angus and Mike's choice to sell the bookstore. "While Jade doesn't have a lot of friends, she has a select few."

"I see she's really found her place here on Marco Island while you've been back this past week." Harry marked off a few more books on the list he had stuck to his clipboard.

"Jade is loving her time here." Mike agreed with Harry. "She's been spending a lot of time at the stables, and she's made some friends who share her love for horses." He frowned, tapping his pen against his chin. "Which is surprising as Jade doesn't usually make friends so quickly."

"But that's a good thing," Harry said, genuinely happy for Jade. "I'm glad she's finding happiness here." He raised an eyebrow. "Maybe you're supposed to be here for her!"

"Nice!" Mike looked at Harry and shook his head. "Use my niece to try and guilt me into not selling the store."

"It was worth a try." Harry shrugged.

"If you're so worried about the store, then you should buy it," Mike suggested.

"Trust me, I've thought about it," Harry admitted. "But Sam would kill me. She's busy planning our retirement with no commitments other than where to sail next."

"You've only just turned fifty," Mike reminded him. "It's a bit early to be planning your retirement."

"Are you kidding me, dude?" Harry stopped and gaped at him. "We've hit the halfway mark to one hundred. For the past twenty to thirty years of our lives, we were like squirrels gathering enough nuts to tie us over for retirement. Now that we've hit fifty, we're taking stock of those nuts to ensure we have enough for our golden years." He raised his brows. "So yeah, we're planning our retirement."

"I've got retirement plans." Mike put some books back on a shelf.

"Yes, but you have a very large supply of nuts for yours." Harry laughed and patted Mike on the back. "We're not all as successful as you, my friend."

"You're successful," Mike reminded him. "You own a chain of hardware stores. So, I reckon you, too, have more than your fair share of nuts gathered for your retirement."

"I also have three kids!" Harry stated. "Two of which are currently at college." He shook his head and blew out a breath. "Do you know how expensive it is to put one child through college?"

"I do, actually," Mike said, pride puffing up his chest. "Jade and I have already started speaking about it."

"We still have another one to put through college." Harry sighed. "You know you've finally gotten the hang of parenting when you secretly hope your lastborn wants to flunk out of school and join a rock band."

Mike laughed at his friend as he thought of Gemma, Harry's youngest child and only daughter, dropping out of school to become a rock star.

"I'm sure Sam would love that." Mike walked into the small kitchen area at the back of the store and took two beers from the refrigerator, handing one to Harry. "Her only girl and her baby, running off to get tattooed and become a drummer."

"I was thinking more of a guitarist." Harry frowned at him. "But trust me, Sam's with me on this one."

They clinked the tops of their beer bottles together before each taking a sip and reminiscing about Angus, their childhood, and the bookstore. Their conversation finally shifted to the cottage next to the bookstore. It had belonged to a woman named Cybill Riley, who had been quite the character in her own right.

"You remember Cybill, right?" Harry asked with a chuckle. "She and Angus were like oil and water. They argued about everything, especially when Angus wanted to buy her cottage to expand the bookstore."

Mike laughed, remembering the countless times he'd witnessed their heated exchanges. "They were like an old married couple, always bickering, but they never seemed to get tired of each other."

"I always wondered if Angus had a soft spot for her," Harry mused. "He was heartbroken when she passed away last year."

"You're more than right about that," Mike admitted. "Did you know they used to date, which was quite serious, too? But then Angus joined the army, and she married Doug Riley." He took a sip of his beer. "Angus never really got over her, even though they always fought. I guess love works in mysterious ways."

Harry nodded, his eyes drifting to the shelves of books. "Maybe that's why they could never figure out what made Angus so ill. He was dying of a broken heart after Cybill was gone."

"It's possible," Mike said quietly, shrugging. "Maybe all those years of bickering were because Cybill had never gotten over Angus either."

They fell into a comfortable silence, each lost in their thoughts about Angus and his impact on their lives. The bookstore felt like a time capsule, preserving the memories of a man who had touched so many lives through his love for books.

"You know, Harry," Mike said, breaking the silence. "I think I need more time to consider selling the bookstore. It's not just a business. It's a legacy, and I don't want to rush into a decision."

Harry smiled, placing a reassuring hand on Mike's shoulder. "Take all the time you need, my friend. Angus would understand and want what's best for you and the bookstore."

The sun bathed the bookstore in a warm golden glow, and Mike couldn't help but feel a sense of peace settling over him. There may be a way to honor his uncle's legacy and keep the bookstore alive. He knew he had a lot to consider. Still, for now, he allowed himself to be immersed in the memories of Angus and the magic of the bookstore that had shaped so many lives, including his own.

The rest of the day passed in a haze of nostalgia and quiet contemplation, and as the day started to dip into late afternoon, Mike made a silent promise to himself and Angus. He would find a way to do right by the legacy of Sully's Corner, just as Angus had done for him and so many others. Mike was about to tell Harry about his decision when he was interrupted by someone ringing the store's front doorbell.

Harry stopped what he was doing and popped his head around the corner of a bookshelf. "You expecting someone?"

"Nope!" Mike shook his head. "I thought maybe you'd ordered pizza."

"I think we should." Harry looked at Mike, who frowned at him, confused. "Order pizza."

Mike nodded in agreement as the doorbell rang again, followed by a knock.

"Hello?" a female voice called. "I can see you in there."

Mike started walking to the front of the store as Harry stepped out from behind a bookshelf with some books in his hand and squinted at the door.

"Hey, isn't that Nicole Scott?" Harry looked questioningly at Mike.

"As in Scott House and Scott's Hotel?" Mike asked Harry, who nodded.

"Yeah, she used to be here all the time. Angus was very fond of her," Harry reminded Mike before grinning at him. "If memory serves me right, you had a giant crush on her."

"What?" Mike spluttered and actually felt his cheeks heat. "I never had a crush on her."

"No, not at all!" Harry raised his eyes and shook his head. "I remember you getting a broken nose from walking into that glass door." He pointed to the open doors. "Because you couldn't take your eyes off her."

"When I was sixteen, I couldn't take my eyes off a lot of teenage girls." Mike gave him a frustrated look.

"Seems like that kinda followed you through manhood too." Harry gave Mike a smug grin. "You know, with the *two* divorces and one broken engagement."

"I get it, Harry!" Mike growled warningly at his friend.

The doorbell rang again.

"You're being rude by staring at me and not letting me in!" Nicky called out as she hit the glass door.

"I agree, you're being rude!" Harry pointed to the glass door.

"Remind me why we're friends again?" Mike hissed and walked toward the front door.

"Because I'm the only one who'll put up with you?" Harry laughed.

Mike's heart slammed into his ribs as he got closer to the door and saw Nicole Scott standing there staring through it at him. She wore a beige cotton shirt with delicate gold and pink roses. It hugged her slender frame and was partially tucked into the hem of her well-worn light blue jeans. While you could see she had matured, her face was still smooth, and her pink bow lips shone with a touch of gloss.

Why did she still have to look so young and beautiful?

He gave himself a mental shake, unlocked the door, and pulled the door open, freezing when his hazel eyes met her big green ones, framed by thick, sooty lashes and perfectly arched natural eyebrows. He swallowed, feeling his throat go dry. Nicole was just as beautiful as he remembered her to be.

"Are you going to stand there staring at me all day, or can I come in?" Nicole's melodic voice drifted toward him and hit him between the eyes, making him realize he was gaping at her.

"Um." Mike cleared his throat. "Sorry, sure, come in."

"Thanks," Nicole said, brushing past him.

Her scent wafted over him, filling his senses, while his skin warmed where she'd brushed him. It wasn't until Harry whispered in her ear that he was jolted back to reality.

"No crush, huh?" Harry patted his shoulder, then walked to Nicky, who was looking around the bookstore. "Nicky Scott, right?"

"Yes, and you're Harry Beckett, Sam's husband." Nicky made the connection between Harry and Nicky's older sister, Lorry.

"That's right." Harry smiled and glanced at Mike. "I believe you know Mike Sullivan, Angus's nephew."

"Yes, I did recognize you." Nicky turned and gave Mike a tight smile. "I came here looking for you after I found out about your uncle." Her eyes darkened with sadness. "I was sorry to hear about his passing. My sincerest condolences. Mr. Sullivan was a truly remarkable man."

"Thank you." Mike's voice sounded gravelly, so he cleared his throat and gave himself another good mental shake. "It's still a big shock."

"I understand that." Nicky nodded. "A sudden loss like that tends to leave one reeling, especially when you have no early warning signs."

"I know this is past due," Harry said to her, "but I'm sorry about the loss of your father."

"Thank you." Nicky turned to Harry before looking at Mike once again. "While I came to pay my respects to you, Mike, I also wanted to discuss the for-sale sign in the window." She pointed to it.

"Oh!" Mike's eyebrows shot up, and he sighed resignedly. He didn't need another lecture on how selling the shop was a bad idea or to hear more stories about his uncle. "If you've come here to try and talk me out of selling." He glanced at Harry. "I've had my fair share of people telling me that already."

"No," Nicky said with a frown marring her brow. "I was going to make you an offer to buy it."

Mike's eyes widened even more to reflect his surprise as he gaped at her.

"Here." Nicky pulled a piece of paper from her jeans pocket. "As I noticed, this was a private sale. I got valuations of the properties in the area and some advice from a property sale advisor as to what the store is worth." She handed him the paper. "This is the offer I would like to make for the store."

Not taking his eyes off her, as he still didn't believe what he'd heard, he reached out and took the paper.

"I hope that's around what you were aiming at selling the store for," Nicky said. "I can pay it all upfront, so there's no waiting for finance."

Mike held the paper in his hands, still staring at her as if in a trance until Harry stepped in and snatched the paper from his hands.

"No, you didn't have a crush on her at all," Harry muttered as he looked at the paper, then elbowed Mike in the ribs. "Wow!" He elbowed Mike again when he still hadn't made a move to look at the offer. "This is—" He looked at Mike. "A very generous offer."

Mike eventually snapped out of his daze and looked at the offer Harry was now holding right in front of his face, and his eyes widened once again as he saw the amount. It was quite a bit over the price he was hoping to get for it.

"Harry's right." Mike finally found his voice again and looked at her, snatching the paper from Harry. "This is a generous offer."

"Have you had any other offers for the store?" Nicky asked him, her brow furrowing deeper.

"No," Harry answered for Mike, who seemed to keep getting tongue-tied. "The for-sale sign only went up yesterday."

"Okay, great." Nicky smiled, and Mike once again felt his heart slam against his rib cage as it lit up her face. "My number is at the bottom of the page." She leaned in to point to it. Her hand brushing against his sent a volt of electricity through his system. "You can call me when you've decided about it."

Mike swallowed and was about to answer when his other best friend, Tom Barnes, walked in carrying three boxes of pizza, more beer, and juice.

"Hey, I brought food and juice for kids and grown-ups." Tom held up the items before walking over to the round table with six chairs surrounding it near the glass doors and putting them on it. "Oh, and I found these two along the way."

"Hey," Sam said, walking in with Jade.

"Hi." Jade waved and walked over to Mike to kiss him on the cheek. "I know what I want for Christmas, Uncle Mike."

"Christmas is six months away, Jay-Jay," Mike pointed out.

"Yes, but you always say it's never too early to put your orders in," Jade reminded him.

"Yes, but that's for other things like school applications." Mike raised his eyebrows.

"Nope, you weren't specific, so no advice take backsies." Jade kissed him again before stopping when she noticed Nicky standing awkwardly between him and Harry.

"Hi, I'm Jade," she introduced herself to Nicky.

"Nicky!" Sam's voice boomed across to them, and she rushed towards their visitor to embrace her. "It's been years since I've seen you."

"Hey, Sam," Nicky said, hugging her back. "You're looking great."

"So do you!" Sam stood back, holding Nicky's hands in hers, and ran her eyes over her. "Lorry told me you were moving back to Marco Island."

"Yes, I got back yesterday," Nick told her. "That's when Hannah noticed the for-sale sign, and here I am making an offer to buy the store."

"You are?" Sam's eyes met Mike's, and her brows raised.

"Yes, Nicky, just arrived and gave it to me," Mike said stupidly. *Did I just say that?*

"I'm starving," Jade groaned and rushed toward the table. "What toppings did you get, Uncle Tom?"

"I know, you eat like a horse for such a tiny thing." Tom smiled at her. "I bought you your own with chicken and barbeque sauce."

"Did you get extra feta on it?" Jade looked at him with narrow eyes.

"Of course, Jay-Jay," Tom told her.

"You're the best." Jade hugged him before scraping a chair back, taking a seat, and getting stuck into the pizza the minute Tom opened the box for her.

"Geez, Mike, are you starving the kid?" Tom stood staring at Jade as she wolfed down the pizza.

"She's an active, growing girl," Mike explained, happy to have his attention taken away from Nicky, who apparently made him become a moron.

"Hi, I'm Tom Barnes," Tom said, walking toward Nicky with a hand held out. "My friends are not the best at introducing people. I sometimes think it's because they forget my name. After all, it's so hard to remember."

Nicky laughed and shook his hand. "Nicky Scott."

"Scott?" Tom frowned as they released their hands. "As in The Scott's Hotel?"

"Yes." Nicky nodded.

"My father is going to be renovating the hotel," Tom told her.

"Oh, I met your father, David, yesterday," Nicky said. "You must be the architect son he told us about."

"Guilty." Tom gave a slight bow.

"Do you want to stay and have some pizza with us?" Jade asked from across the room.

"That's very kind of you to offer," Nicky said. "But I've got plans." She looked at her wristwatch. "Which, if I don't leave now, I'm going to be late for." She smiled at Tom. "It was nice to meet you."

"Likewise." Tom's smile widened, and Mike's eyes narrowed suspiciously at his friend.

"Are you sure you can't change your plans and stay?" Sam tried to entice her, glancing pointedly around the store. "I know how much you love spending time in this place."

"As tempting as that sounds," Nicky laughed, "I have to go."

She turned to Mike and said, "Call me when you've made a decision." She looked at Harry. "It was good to see you again, Harry."

With that, Nicole left the store, and Mike stared after her, finding himself having to suppress the urge to try and make her stay for pizza as he wondered where she was rushing off to. Mike gave himself yet another mental shake and stern talking to before he managed to make himself move so his friends wouldn't think he was a complete idiot.

"Nope, you definitely *never* had a crush on her. I think you may not have found the right one because you let her get away when you were sixteen." Harry slapped Mike on the back before walking toward the pizza, chuckling.

CHAPTER 4

The sun had begun its descent, casting a warm golden hue over Tigertail Beach as Nicky walked back from Sully's Corner to Scott House. The rhythmic sound of waves crashing against the shore created a soothing backdrop for her thoughts. Her stomach was in knots about the offer she'd made to Mike for the bookstore. Buying the store now seemed like an impulsive decision she'd made at the height of excitement after Nicky and Hannah saw the for-sale sign in the store window.

Nicky hadn't allowed herself the chance to talk herself out of making an offer. Instead, she'd phoned her best friend, Mandy Oliver, now a real estate agent in Naples, for advice and what to offer. Mandy had given Nicky a ballpark figure and asked her to wait a few days before making an offer. Mandy would be back in Marco Island in a few days and could do a proper evaluation. But Nicky knew if she'd waited even a few more hours, she'd probably have talked herself out of her decision. So, Nicky took a breath, wrote the offer on a piece of paper with her number, and walked to the store to put in her offer.

Sully's Corner held a strong sense of nostalgia for Nicky. As a girl, she often pictured herself owning Sully's Corner. In her mind, she went back to when she'd told Mr. Sullivan how she'd take over his store but expand it to include a coffee shop that maybe sold some trinkets. Mr. Sullivan had been swept up in her musings and admitted that he'd always pictured putting up a beach hut leading from the store. He wanted to sell refreshments and rent beach chairs, beach game items, etc.

Nicky stopped for a second and let her eyes scan the beach. She looked back to where Sully's Corner was perched in the perfect position, with its back deck nearly reaching the sand. She could picture selling soft-serve ice cream, sodas, water, juice, and other summer refreshments. Maybe in the winter, Nicky could replace those refreshments with winter warmers. She could even have it as a juice bar for runners, cyclists, and walkers. Nicky smiled as her heart fluttered once again with a mixture of excitement over having put in an offer, fear that she may have done the rashest thing of her life, and anxiety over whether or not Mike would accept her offer.

Nicky blew out a breath as she turned to carry on home. Her thoughts meandered through the labyrinth of the past six months of her life. Her steps took her across the sandy expanse of Tigertail Beach, a route she'd taken countless times during her childhood and teenage years. This beach held a special place in her heart, offering solace and tranquility whenever life became overwhelming. Over the years, Tigertail Beach had become her confidant, with the sand offering comfort and the sea soothing her soul.

Lost in her contemplations, Nicky nearly didn't notice a figure sitting a little distance away. By the shake of her shoulders and how the young woman held her head, it looked like she was weeping. When Nicky first saw the woman, it was like seeing a haunting reminder of the many times she'd sat on the beach, sobbing into her hands. Nicky stopped walking and hesitated for a moment, unsure whether or not to approach the young woman. As Nicky took a few steps closer, she could see the woman was pregnant, and something about her pulled at Nicky's heartstrings.

Following her heart and intuition, Nicky cautiously approached her.

"Hi," Nicky said gently. Her heart was bleeding for the young woman as she looked up at Nicky with tear-streaked cheeks. Nicky recognized the look of despair in the woman's eyes. "Are you okay?"

The young woman's eyes were red and puffy from crying. She sucked in a shaky breath and gave a faint nod. "I'm... I'm fine."

"You don't look fine." Nicky settled down beside her in the sand, offering a sympathetic smile. "You look like someone far too young to be battling with all the despair I see in your eyes."

The young woman hiccupped, wiping away a tear, and sighed. "It's just... my life feels like it's falling apart."

Nicky's empathy deepened. "Do you want to talk about it?" She gave her a warm smile. "Sometimes speaking to a stranger helps because they don't have any preconceived opinions about you." She tilted her head, looking at the young woman. "Sharing your burdens with someone can also make them feel a little lighter."

The young woman hesitated for a moment before letting out a shaky breath. "I don't even know where to start. Everything feels like a mess."

"How about with introductions?" Nicky held out her hand. "I'm Nicky."

The young woman gave her a small, appreciative smile. "My name's Megan."

"It's nice to meet you, Megan," she replied, as Megan took her hand and shook it.

"It's nice to meet you, Nicky." Megan let go of Nicky's hand and rubbed her extended belly. "Oh, she's kicking again."

"Oh!" Nicky's eyes widened as she saw Megan's pink t-shirt do a small jump.

"Here." Megan grabbed Nicky's hand and put it on her stomach.

Nicky was amazed to feel a few thumps against her palm as if the baby was trying to push her hand away.

"Goodness, that's quite a kick!" Nicky laughed, pulling her hand away. "How far along are you?"

"Just over eight months." Megan ran her hands over her protruding belly, sadness darkening her eyes. "And what an emotional time it's been."

"Pregnancy plays havoc with a woman's emotions," Nicky sympathized.

Megan's shoulders sagged and she looked out at the horizon. "It does, and it seems to intensify all the other problems around you."

"I find the best way to deal with my problems is to talk them out." Nicky encouraged her to open up. Megan was clearly carrying the weight of her world on her shoulders. "What about your family?" She looked at Megan.

"I don't have any left," Megan murmured. "My grandmother, who raised me since I was twelve, died a year ago." She sucked in a shaky breath. "And my boyfriend—my ex-boyfriend now—left me when he found out I was pregnant." She swallowed and swiped at a fresh tear rolling down her cheek. "I thought he loved me, but I guess I was wrong." She shook her head. "As soon as my small inheritance dried up, he was out the door faster than a striking rattlesnake and, within a week, had moved in with his new girlfriend."

"What a douche!" Megan hissed, her brows knitting together, her heart going out to her. "I'm so sorry to hear that. That must be really tough."

Megan nodded, her eyes brimming with more fresh tears. "And then there's the cottage. My grandmother owned it, and now it's mine. But I'm just a college student with no idea how to run a house, let alone look after all the maintenance." Her eyes met Nicky's. "I don't know what to do with it, but it's got bills piling up, and I can't afford it." She looked at her stomach once again. "I'll be without utilities if I don't find a summer job soon."

Nicky listened with genuine empathy. "That sounds like a lot to handle."

"It is," Megan admitted, her voice breaking. "And on top of everything, the funds I had for college got cut off." Her eyes shot to Nicky's again. "My mother, who passed away seven years ago, had a small pension fund that paid for my college. I was supposed to start again in the fall, but now I don't know how I'll manage."

Nicky could feel the weight of Megan's despair, and she leaned closer. "Megan, I know things seem overwhelming right now, but you're not alone. There are people who can help you." She pulled her knees up and wrapped her arms around them. "You could get a scholarship or a student loan." Her eyes widened with a thought. "If you own your grandmother's cottage, you could look into taking a loan against it."

Megan wiped away another tear, her gaze distant. "I don't even know where to begin."

Nicky placed a comforting hand on Megan's shoulder. "You can start by talking to someone about your options. Some organizations offer support to pregnant women and students in difficult situations."

Megan's eyes met Nicky's, a glimmer of hope emerging amidst her distress. "Do you know any of them?"

Nicky nodded, feeling a twinge of guilt for her white lie, and made a mental note to find out what she could do for Megan when she got home. "Yes, I do. And I'll make a list for you when I get home."

Megan let out a shaky breath as she swatted away some more tears. "Thank you, Nicky." She gave Nicky a watery smile. "Do you believe in fate?"

"For a long time, I didn't," Nicky admitted. "I kept thinking that if the series of events happening to me was fate somehow trying to redirect my life, then fate was a sadistic jerk who I must've angered at some point in my life without even knowing it."

Megan laughed and wiped her nose on her bedraggled tissue. "That's how I felt until you sat beside me on the sand and chased away that dark cloud that's been following me lately."

"Then maybe fate is doing something nice for you, and I'm glad I could be part of it," Nicky said.

"I wasn't going to come out here today." Megan looked at the water. "But I swear I could hear my grandmother telling me we're lucky to live so close to the sea. Every day, we need to take advantage of that and go outside, even for a minute, to breathe in the salty air. To refresh our souls and get a few minutes of vitamin D to soak into our skin."

"Your grandmother sounded like a wise woman," Nicky told her.

"She was." Megan's head dropped, as did her voice, at the mention of her grandmother. "I miss her so much." She fiddled with her fingers. "That's why I decided to get out into the fresh air and sit in her favorite spot."

"Ah," Nicky said with a nod. "I also have a favorite spot on this beach." She pointed further down the beach to where they could see the profile of Scott's Hotel. "I thought of it as an old friend where I'd sit and tell my troubles to the wind, sand, and ocean."

"Are you Nicky Scott?" Megan's eyes widened in realization.

"Yes." Nicky sighed. "That's me."

"I remember you." Megan smiled. "My mother used to work for your father." Her smile faded, and her eyes darkened. "I'm sorry about his passing."

"Thank you," Nicky said, her mind ticking over as she pulled up a memory from a long time ago and suddenly realized who Megan was. "Are you Jackie Riley's Nutmeg?"

"Wow!" Megan laughed. "I haven't heard that nickname in years."

"Oh, my goodness," Nicky said, her eyes roving over Megan's face. "Yes, I see it now." Then, another thought struck her. "Did you say your grandmother passed away?" Her brow creased a bit more. "Cybill's gone?"

"Yes." Megan swallowed and nodded, her eyes getting misty. "She hadn't been well for about six months before she died."

"I'm so sorry, Megan." Nicky's voice was low and full of compassion. "Your grandmother was such a force of nature and so fit for her age."

"That was before she had a bad fall and shattered her hip," Megan explained. "After the operation, she was never the same."

"What a shame." Nicky shook her head, then looked worriedly at Megan. "Are you okay on your own at the cottage?"

"I've been staying there since summer vacation began," Megan told her. "Mike Sullivan, Mr. Sullivan, from the bookstore's nephew, is staying at Sullivan's Cottage next to mine." She looked around. "He's been great, and Sam Beckett calls on me all the time as well."

"That's good to know," Nicky said.

"I don't know if you heard, but Mr. Sullivan passed away six months ago." Megan wiped the stray tears from her cheeks. "There's been so much loss and pain over the past year."

"I know about Mr. Sullivan," Nicky answered. "I was coming from the bookstore when I found you." She smiled. "I've put in an offer to buy the store."

"Oh, that's amazing!" Megan's eyes widened with joy. "Mr. Sullivan would be pleased for you to have his store." She smiled. "He spoke about you quite a bit about how you were his best customer in his store nearly every day, curling up on the armchair near the glass door with your nose in a book."

"That was me!" Nicky confirmed. "I did love that store, and between you and me, I always dreamed of owning it one day."

"Does this mean you're moving back to Marco Island?" Megan asked her. "I'm sure Mr. Sullivan said something about you living in Miami."

"I moved back yesterday, as a matter of fact." Nicky dusted the sand off her hands. "As soon as I drove in, I saw the for-sale sign in the bookstore window."

"Well, I'm glad you did." Megan gave Nicky's arm a squeeze. "And I think you should start believing in fate again because I think it led you back home to Marco Island for a reason." She looked toward the bookstore. "One of them being to buy the bookstore, the other to help a distressed nineteen-year-old realize that talking really does help, and I'm sure the other reasons will become obvious as the days unfold."

"I guess so!" Nicky pursed her lips and nodded before looking at Megan. "Say, what are you doing for dinner?"

"Nothing. I was going to boil an egg or something." Megan shrugged. "I hadn't really thought about it."

"You can't just have a boiled egg and bread!" Nicky shuddered. "Why don't you come to my house for dinner?" She glanced at the Scotts House. "My mother is cooking tonight, and she cooks enough to feed the whole of Marco Island."

"I don't want to put anyone out." Megan looked toward the Scott properties.

"Nonsense!" Nicky waved her concern off. "Besides, my grandmother would love someone to fuss over."

"If you're sure." Megan's eyes searched Nicky's.

"Come on." Nicky pushed herself to her feet and dusted the sand off, holding out her hands to help Megan up.

"Thanks," Megan puffed as she stood. "The heavier I get, the harder it is to get up off the ground."

"I can imagine." Nicky couldn't help the catch in her voice and shook the pang of pain away.

"Thank you, Nicky." Megan gave her a small smile, her vulnerability and gratitude shining through. "Talking to you has made me feel a bit better."

"I'm glad to hear that," Nicky replied, a warm smile of her own forming. "Remember, you're stronger than you think, Megan." She put her arm around Megan's narrow shoulders as they walked toward Scott House. "Sometimes we just need someone to remind us of that."

As the sun dipped lower on the horizon, casting hues of orange and pink across the sky, they walked in companionable silence, sharing a bond of empathy. In the background, the waves continued their rhythmic dance, a reminder of the constancy of nature amid life's uncertainties.

Nicky and Megan had no sooner stepped onto the small boardwalk that led to the Scott's Hotel and Scott House when Nelly Scott, Nicky's grandmother, rushed out to greet them.

"Goodness, is that Megan Riley?" Nelly pulled Megan into a warm embrace. "Hello, honey, how are you?"

"Hello, Mrs. Scott." Megan smiled shyly. "I'm a lot better after Nicky found me."

Nelly's brows shot up as she looked inquiringly at Nicky.

"I was out walking on the beach," Nicky explained. "I invited Megan for dinner."

"I hope that's okay?" Megan asked quickly.

"Of course," Nelly said emphatically. "I'm so glad she did too. Pat always makes way too much food, and then we have to freeze it and end up eating for weeks to come."

The three women walked into Scott House as Pat came out from the kitchen to greet them.

"Megan, welcome," Pat said, holding out her arms for a hug.

Pat embraced Megan and led them through the back lounge, which opened onto the patio that faced the sea.

"Would you like some tea?" Nelly asked Megan, who nodded. "Is herbal tea okay?"

Megan nodded before sitting on one of the small sofas across from Nicky as Nelly and Pat disappeared back into the kitchen.

"Do you have children, Nicky?" Megan asked, unaware of the raw nerve she'd hit.

"No." Was all Nicky could manage to get out with a swift shake of her head and her mind racing to pick another subject to talk about. But for some reason, her tongue got stuck on babies. "You mentioned you were having a girl back on the beach."

"Yes." Megan nodded and rubbed her belly.

"Have you thought of names?" Nicky's mind screamed, *Change the subject!* But she couldn't stop the words that tumbled from her mouth.

"No." Megan shook her head, and her eyes darkened with emotion. Before she said the next words, Nicky knew what Megan was about to say. "I don't think I should." She cleared her throat, and her eyes shone with a mixture of pain and guilt. "I'm only nineteen and want to go to college." She looked at her stomach, cradling it protectively. "Right now, I'm not in any position to give my daughter the life she deserves." She lifted her teary eyes to Nicky. Her voice was hoarse with emotion. "I'm not sure I'm going to keep her."

CHAPTER 5

The sun was already making its descent beyond the horizon as Mike laced up his running shoes before hitting the sand. It was his routine, his way of clearing his mind and rejuvenating himself after a long day of sorting through the remnants of his uncle's life. The sand beneath his feet was soft, and he imagined it would be cool, a stark contrast to the warmth of the day that was fading into the evening.

As he picked up the pace, his breathing fell into rhythm with the crashing waves. It was a familiar melody that he had come to cherish during his time on Marco Island. The beach was relatively empty at this hour, a serene expanse that offered a sense of solitude, allowing him to clear his mind. The stress of the day melted away with each stride until he reached the end of the beach and turned around to retrace his steps.

Mike was adjusting his stopwatch and congratulating himself on making his best time yet as he strode down the small path to his uncle's cottage. He wasn't looking where he was going and collided with a figure hurrying out the gate of Riley Cottage that sat beside his uncle's.

"Watch out!" Mike's voice was sharp as he lunged forward, his hand extending to prevent a collision.

A jolt of surprise zapped through Mike, and his eyes widened in surprise as they met the startled ones of Nicky Scott. His already rapidly beating heart sprung into overdrive, making his fingers clench a little too tightly and dig into the flesh of the person's upper arms.

"Ow!" Nicky hissed, flinching and twisting out of his grip. "Watch where you're going."

Nicky took a step back and stumbled, her hands flailing out in front of her, which Mike instinctively reached out and caught, once again steadying her. Another zap from touch jolted through him—a sensation he hadn't anticipated—when her fingers curled into his.

"Whoa!" Mike exclaimed, holding onto her hands as she righted herself, and their eyes met.

For a moment, Mike was frozen. His eyes locked with hers. He had almost knocked her over, yet something about how she looked at him—half startled, half amused—struck a chord within him.

"Sorry about that," he managed to say, his voice rougher than intended.

She blinked, her gaze moving from his face to his hands still holding hers. "No problem. I should've been more careful exiting a gate without turn signals."

She gave a soft laugh. The sound sent a warm shiver up his spine, and his throat went dry as her smile transformed her and lit up her green eyes, making all thoughts leave his head and his tongue unable to form any words. An awkward silence fell between them as Mike stood gaping as if transfixed by her.

It wasn't until she pulled her hands from his that he realized he was still holding them and had to resist the urge to clamp down on her hands to not let them go. His palms still tingled with the feeling of hers, and an image of water slipping through his fingers flashed through his mind. Mike gave himself a mental shake, closed his mouth, and cleared his throat.

"Are you okay?" he asked, his tone as composed as he could manage while his addled brain tried to right itself with no help from his hyperactive heart and tongue that was twisted in knots.

She nodded, offering a faint smile. "Yeah, thanks for the save."

Their eyes met once again, and although he didn't think it possible at the moment, Mike's pulse quickened. He wasn't sure what the heck was going on with him, as he'd always been confident around women. Still, something about her—her eyes, the way she carried herself—left him feeling like a tongue-tied sixteen-year-old with a crush on the hottest girl in school.

"Late evening run?" she asked, her voice breaking another awkward silence.

He nodded, grateful for the conversation starter. "Yeah, I usually run twice a day when I'm here. Early morning and at night." *Did she need to know that?* He admonished himself.

Her brows lifted slightly. Her curiosity was evident, mixed with amusement, in her expression. "Twice a day? That's impressive dedication."

Mike once again found himself at a loss for words, a rare occurrence for him. He watched as she shifted her weight, a strand of hair catching the fading light.

"Megan tells me you're staying at your uncle's cottage." Nicky made casual conversation.

Mike nodded, finding his voice once more. "Yeah, I live in the cottage right next door to Megan's." *Did I just say that?* He had to stop the urge to slap himself on the forehead over his stupidity.

Her eyes flickered with amusement for a second, and she pointed toward Scott House as he was standing with his back to it. "I should get going."

Mike managed a half-smile, though his mind still grappled with the unexpected encounter. "Likewise." *Likewise? Pull yourself together, man, before she thinks you're a complete moron.*

"Well, then, goodnight, Mike," Nicky said, stepping around them. "I hope to hear from you soon about my offer for the bookstore."

With that, she started to walk off. Mike found himself watching her retreating figure. He couldn't explain the odd pull he felt toward her—a sense that his life was about to be turned upside down.

"Geez Louise, that was so hard to watch." Jade's teasing voice snapped him out of his daze.

Mike turned to see her leaning against the cottage gate with a mug between her hands. Her eyes danced with amusement.

Mike rolled his eyes, though his thoughts lingered on the encounter. "What are you talking about?"

"I've never seen you like that before." Jade chuckled, clearly enjoying his discomfort. "Uncle Mike, I could practically feel the awkwardness from here."

He sighed and pushed the gate open, with her standing on it for a ride. "You're imagining things."

Jade's grin only widened. "Sure, Uncle Mike. Whatever you say."

"You shouldn't be eavesdropping on other people's conversations." Mike took the hand towel from the veranda railing as he walked into the house, with Jade following him.

"I wouldn't call whatever that was a conversation." Jade laughed as he turned and threw his sweaty towel at her, which she dodged.

"Shouldn't you be bathing and getting ready for bed?" Mike asked her as they walked into the kitchen, and he pulled a bottle of water from the refrigerator.

"Nope, it's summer vacation, and I don't have to be in bed until at least twelve." Jade gave him a smug look. "As per your rules."

"I miss the days when your vacation curfew was nine o'clock." Mike sighed.

"I honestly don't know why you even bother with your curfew rules." Jade sipped her hot chocolate. "You never enforce them."

"I do during school days," Mike pointed out before downing the rest of the water. "Weren't you going to tell me about this horse you want to buy?"

"Clever!" Jade nodded, raising one brow. "Tempt me into another conversation to avoid further embarrassment over you nearly knocking Nicky Scott off her feet."

"This is your last chance to discuss the horse!" Mike closed the bottle of water and threw it into the recycling bin.

"Fine!" Jade relented, pulling out a chair from the small round table perched in the center of the kitchen. "His name is Midnight."

"His name?" Mike's eyes narrowed as he sat in a chair facing her. "Is he a gelding?"

"Wait!" Jade held up both her hands. "Can I finish telling you about him before you go all judgey about my choice?"

"If you mean all judgey over not wanting you to be riding a stallion, then no, you can't finish telling me about him." Mike leaned his elbows on the table. "You need a nice, docile mare or gelding."

"Won't you please hear me out?" Jade argued. "Midnight is an ex-racehorse that was retired because he hurt his leg."

"Oh, so you want a crippled stallion?" Mike sat back and folded his arms across his chest, trying not to let his mind wander back to his run-in with Nicole.

"Midnight is not crippled!" Jade's voice was filled with impatience. "You're deliberately being difficult, aren't you?"

"No, honey." Mike shook his head. "I want to see the horse first." His eyes met her blue ones, which were so like her mother's. "We also made a deal that you'd find three or four that you liked, and we'd make a choice together."

"So, I can get a horse?" Jade suddenly said.

"Wait, let me rephrase that." Mike held up his hand.

"Nope, too late. No take backsies." Jade grinned and clapped her hands before flying off her chair to hug and kiss him on the cheek. "Thank you, Uncle Mike. You're my favorite uncle."

"I'm your only uncle," Mike reminded her with a grin. "And I thought when we discussed this earlier, I said that I was open to considering the possibility of you getting a horse."

"No, you didn't say that." Jade shook her head and glanced at the large silver clock over the kitchen door. "Oh, my show's about to come on."

"Oh, so our conversation is over?" Mike's eyebrows shot up.

"Yes... Wait, no." Jade turned back toward him after starting to head for the living room. "Can we go to the stables tomorrow?"

"Sure, why not?" Mike said, smiling.

Being out at the horse ranch on the outskirts of town would get his mind off the store, his decision to sell it, and mostly Nicky. At least at the ranch, he wouldn't stand a chance of running into her again and making a complete dolt of himself.

"Great!" Jade kissed his cheek again before hurrying out the door and calling over her shoulder. "Oh, I've already bathed, but some hot water should be left for your shower."

Mike sighed as he knew Jade's interpretation of leaving him some hot water was him taking a lukewarm to cold shower. He heard the television go on and took that as his cue to shower. Standing under the warm spray, Mike reflected on the day's events. He still couldn't believe he'd had two encounters with Nicky that day. Mike couldn't believe how both encounters had taken him by surprise, and he cringed inwardly as he remembered them. He had never been one to stumble over his words, and yet Nicky had left him tongue-tied and gaping like a goldfish in a bowl. He leaned his arms against the shower wall, his thoughts drifting back to her.

The following day, after a restless night of dreams that tormented him with images of Nicky and the bookstore, Mike woke up with a headache. After a good stretch and run, he felt a lot better. Jade convinced him to go to the stables in the morning to join Harry, Sam, and their daughter Gemma for a trail ride.

On the way to Bailey's Horse Ranch and Stables, they stopped at Jade's favorite café for breakfast and arrived at the ranch just after ten. Jade chose his horse for him, and it was no surprise that it was Midnight. There was no doubting how beautiful the horse was. As per his name, Midnight had an inky black coat that shone and glinted in the sun. He stood seventeen hands high with long, powerful legs and a full mane.

They were saddled up when Harry, Sam, and Gemma arrived. Their horses, which they stabled at the ranch, had been saddled for them.

"Howdy," Harry joked, loving anything referencing cowboys, and grinned pointedly at Mike. "I see you're attempting to go horseback riding again."

"I can ride!" Mike said defensively. "I took lessons for a year, if you remember?"

"Uh-huh!" Harry nodded, skillfully mounting his horse, Robbins, that he stabled at the ranch. "Of course, I remember." He walked Robbins over to where Mike was sitting awkwardly on Midnight. "Why on earth are you riding Midnight?"

"Because Jade wants me to test drive him." Mike patted the fidgety horse's neck and had to stop himself from jumping as the horse's skin shivered. He hated it when it did that. It gave him the creeps. "She wants to buy him."

"He's not a car." Harry shook his head, grinning as he noted Mike getting creeped out.

"I know he's not a car," Mike breathed and muttered, "Although I really wish he was."

"You may want to reconsider riding Midnight," Harry suggested. "He's a wonderful horse, but with an experienced rider like Jade, Sam, Gemma, or me."

"I can ride!" Mike stipulated again, frustrated that his best friend didn't trust his abilities to ride a darn horse. "I've got experience."

"Hi, Mike," Sam greeted him, riding her roan mare, Crispin, over to them. "I see you've chosen to ride Midnight."

"Yes," Mike said. "And, before you say anything, I can ride, and I'm going to be fine riding Midnight."

"I wasn't going to say that," Sam told him. "I was just going to say that Hannah Scott was a little annoyed that someone else was riding her favorite horse."

"Scott?" Mike's heart jolted in his chest, and his whole body vibrated. "She's here?"

"Yes, Hannah, Steph, Lorry, and Nicky are going to be riding the trail with us." Sam's words sent shock waves zinging through him.

"Don't the Scotts have their own horses?" Harry asked his wife.

"Yes, and Midnight's one of them," Sam reminded him. "Lorry's the one selling Midnight."

"Oh, well, they'll be pleased to know that Mike's taking him for a test drive," Harry teased Mike.

"You're thinking of buying Midnight?" Sam's eyes widened in surprise. "Are you sure?" She looked from Mike to the horse, which was getting a little edgy. "He's a lovely animal and gentle."

"But?" Mike looked at her questioningly with raised brows.

"He's more for an experienced rider," Sam said. "Like Jade."

"I was thinking of buying him for Jade, and that's why I'm riding him," Mike told them. "I'm worried about her riding a stallion."

"Then you'll be pleased to know that Midnight is a gelding." Nicky's voice had Mike nearly falling out of the saddle as she rode up beside him.

She was on a beautiful silver horse that was just as tall as Midnight. It was like no horse he'd seen before. The horse's coat was silver with a metallic sheen that shone in the sunlight. The horse had a black face with a white diamond on its forehead. Its ears, mane, tail, and elegant legs were also a silky black—the horse was as striking as the woman riding him.

"But I thought Midnight was a racehorse?" Mike's mind turned to pudding once again as he stared at Nicky poised on the large stallion as if she were born in the saddle.

"Most racehorses are gelded to make them better able to focus on racing," Nicky explained, and he noticed she did so without being condescending, unlike his friend.

"Oh, really?" Mike asked, although he'd only just remembered that bit of information the moment she'd started to explain it to him.

"Yes, Midnight's gelded and a great horse." Nicky leaned over and stroked the animal. "Hey, boy." She smiled at Mike, and he swallowed as he watched her lean over and pat her horse's neck. "Storm Chaser is a stallion."

Midnight, who had felt Mike was nervous of him and had been prancing, instantly calmed down when Nicky stroked him.

Good grief, even the horse is affected by her. Mike felt a little better knowing he wasn't the only one affected by Nicky Scott.

Nicky was greeted by Jade and the Beckett family as her three sisters joined her. They were all riding horses owned by the Scotts, two of which they were also selling. Mike wanted to ask why they were suddenly selling three horses, but his niece, riding Arrow, joined them.

"Hi, Nicky, it's nice to see you again." Jade greeted Nicky, casting a cheeky grin at Mike and ignoring his warning scowl. "I love your horse."

"I do, too," Nicky told her. "Sam tells me you've become quite the accomplished rider."

"I'm trying, as I love horseback riding." Jade's grin broadened at the praise.

"Well, I must say you look like a natural on a horse," Nicky complimented her.

"She does, doesn't she?" Mike agreed proudly.

"How long have you been riding for, Mike?" Nicky asked him.

"Oh, a while," Mike hedged.

"Awesome!" Nicky smiled. "I've been wanting to go check out Pan's Waterfall again." She looked from Mike to Jade. "But my sisters don't want to ride that far today. Would you two like to come with me?" She pointed to her saddlebags. "I have enough here to make a small picnic."

"I'd love to," Jade beamed, looking at Mike. "Oh, please, can we?"

"Sure, why not?" Mike agreed, swallowing a lump of panic, knowing how far Pan's Waterfall was.

"We don't mind riding with you either," Harry said, inviting himself and his family with them. "Sam has enough food on Mischa, our

73

saddle horse. We were going to invite you all for a picnic with us anyway."

"That's even better," Nicky said, looking toward her sisters. "Are you three sure you can't join us?"

"We have to get back to work," Steph said, looking disappointed. "You know how much I love going to Pan's Waterfall."

"I have to spend some time with Mom before I head back to Palm Beach tomorrow," Hannah said.

"Sorry, I have to get back to work as well." Lorry sighed.

"Well, then it looks like it's just the six of us for the picnic," Sam said before kicking her horse into a walk to join Lorry, Gemma, Hannah, and Steph, who were going to lead the first part of the trail.

"I'll catch you later," Nicky said to Mike, gave Harry a nod, and trotted off.

"I'm going to join them up front with Gemma," Jade said, giving Mike a worried look. "Are you going to be okay riding at the back with Uncle Harry and Mischa?"

"Of course," Mike said, trying to convince himself as well. "You go ahead, sweetheart."

Jade took off, and Mike turned to see Harry shaking his head at him.

"Why did you lie to Nicky about being able to ride?" Harry asked him as they kicked the horse into a walk, with Mischa being led by Harry.

"I didn't lie," Mike hissed, tired of people putting his riding skills down. "I simply didn't tell her the whole truth."

"Yes, I just said that," Harry pointed out. "You lied."

They rode behind the woman, whom they could hear laughing and chatting ahead of them.

"I didn't lie. I may have slightly misled her," Mike admitted.

"You must be relieved, though," Harry said, and Mike glanced at him, confused.

"About?" Mike's brows knitted together.

"About Nicky not being too concerned about you plowing her down last night." Harry started to chuckle as he saw Mike swear beneath his breath.

"Jade told you about that?" Mike hissed.

"No, it wasn't Jade." Harry's chuckle turned into a laugh.

"Jade was the only one around at the time." Mike's eyes narrowed suspiciously.

"Nope, Sam witnessed the whole thing." Harry's words made Mike go cold. "She was on her way to check on Megan."

"Great!" Mike hissed and accidentally kicked Midnight, spurring him into a gallop.

Mike nearly fell off with the force at which the horse took off, and he found himself hanging on for his life with Harry shouting after him.

"Rein him in!" Harry called.

After that, everything went by in a blur because of the speed at which Mike found himself flying over the ground. He had no idea where she came from, but he was flooded with relief when Nicky appeared beside him and stopped Midnight.

"Whoa, boy!" Nicky called to Midnight as she skillfully managed to reign the rampaging horse in while not losing her balance in her saddle. "Whoa!" When Midnight stopped and pranced a bit, Mike breathed a sigh of relief, and Nicky asked him. "Are you okay?"

"Humiliated!" Mike admitted, "but I'm fine," and he grinned at her as he realized that although he was speeding out of control on top of a powerful animal, it was exhilarating. "And oddly exhilarated at the same time."

"That's the adrenaline and the incredible feeling of flying across the land." Nicky smiled. "It's like no feeling on earth."

"It really is." Mike agreed. "I'm sorry you had to rush after me."

He'd galloped a horse before but had never gone as fast as that.

"Are you kidding?" Nicky's eyes shone, and that's when he realized she'd loved getting her horse up to a high speed after him. "Except for the worry that something might happen to you or Midnight, Storm Chaser and I were thrilled to come after you."

"He's a beautiful horse." Mike looked pointedly at the horse as his heart rate finally slowed.

"I know. My father left him to me." Nicky's voice caught, and her eyes clouded with emotion.

"Everything alright here?" Harry came riding up to them. His face was white with worry.

"Yes, he's fine," Nicky assured Harry.

"You're lucky Nicky was here," Harry grumbled at Mike. "She's the most accomplished rider out of all of us."

"He's fine," Nicky assured Harry again. "Mike was handling Midnight really well and had basically stopped him by the time I got near them."

"Thank goodness for Storm Chaser," Harry said, running a hand through his hair and glancing at the other horses, making their way toward them. "None of our horses would've been able to catch Midnight."

"None of us would've been able to, even if we were on a horse as fast as Midnight," Hannah commented. "I knew I should've taken

Midnight." She smiled warmly at Mike. "Not that I doubt your riding abilities, but Midnight has a hair trigger when he needs a good run."

"He hasn't been out on the trail for a few weeks to have a good run," Lorry explained.

"So basically, what my friends are trying to tell you, Mike," Sam said, giving Harry a warning look, "before my husband teases you, is that you were basically handed a loaded gun!"

"Geez, did you have to tell him that?" Jade said, rolling her eyes as she and Gemma caught up to them. "I'm trying to get my uncle to buy him for me."

"Why do you want Midnight so badly?" Mike asked her.

"Because he and I understand each other," Jade surprised him by saying. "Do you want to swap horses for the rest of the ride, Uncle Mike?"

"I'm not sure I want you riding him, sweetheart," Mike said honestly, grateful that no one was making him feel like a complete idiot for his wild horseback ride.

"But Uncle Mike," Jade began, but he cut her off.

"I'm sorry, honey, but I think he's just too much for you." Mike's voice brooked no argument. "Now, shall we continue our trail ride?"

CHAPTER 6

Nicky could see that Midnight was still itching to stretch his powerful legs, and she'd been surprised to find a novice riding on his back. Nicky smiled to herself. She knew Mike was trying hard, but she could see he wasn't as confident as he was trying to appear in the saddle.

"Mike, do you mind if I take Midnight for a while?" Nicky offered. "I can exercise him, and you'll see how gentle he can be once he's been exercised."

"You want me to ride *your* horse?" Mike's eyes widened as he gaped at the stallion Nicky was perched on.

"I promise you, Storm Chaser won't take off at the spur of the moment," Nicky promised. "He's a lot more disciplined than Midnight."

"Okay!" Mike's eyes narrowed as he watched Nicky dismount, and he did the same.

Nicky smiled warmly at Mike as Harry slid out of his saddle to hold Storm Chaser while Mike climbed into the saddle.

"I'll keep an eye on them," Harry promised, and Nicky didn't miss the look the two men exchanged.

"I'll meet you at Pan's Waterfall," Nicky told them.

She confidently swung into the saddle and felt Midnight give a little prance of excitement, knowing he was about to do what he loved—run. With a gentle nudge and a soft word of encouragement, they were off. The sensation was exhilarating as they surged forward, the horse's powerful muscles propelling them across the open fields. The wind whipped through Nicky's hair, tugging at loose strands and bringing a sense of liberation. The scenery around them was a picturesque panorama of rolling hills and vibrant wildflowers, all a blur as they raced forward. Nicky leaned into Midnight's rhythmic stride, feeling the horse's energy surge beneath her. Together, they were a force of nature, a harmonious blend of rider and steed, as they galloped toward Pan's Waterfall.

·❤·❤·❤·❤·❤·

"She's magnificent," Mike murmured, watching Nicky handle the powerful beast with ease as horse and rider melded into the perfect team, disappearing over the horizon.

"That she is!" Harry agreed with a chuckle and glanced at the horse walking sedately with Mike perched on top. "How does it feel to be seated on the infamous Storm Chaser?"

"Surprisingly easy to ride, and I feel more at ease on him than I did on Midnight," Mike admitted. "It's like admiring a pedigree supercar from afar and not being sure if you could handle it, but you start to drive it, and it handles like a dream."

"Are you comparing a racehorse to an Italian sports car?" Harry looked at him in disbelief.

"I believe I am." Mike laughed and confidently leaned forward to pat Storm Chaser on the neck. "He's a beautiful animal." He looked at the high glossy sheen of the horse's coat. "It's like his coat has a pearly sheen to it."

"That breed is known for its shiny coat," Harry told him. "It's an Akhal-Teke."

"I'll take your word for it." Mike laughed.

There were only a few breeds he knew about, and those were quarter horses, Appaloosas, Arabians, and Paint horses. Mike doubted he'd even remember that breed's name, let alone know how to pronounce it.

"Nicky must like you," Harry pointed out, surprising Mike.

"Why would you say that?" Mike frowned.

"Nicky apparently doesn't let *anyone* ride Storm Chaser," Harry explained. "He was her father's horse, and he left Storm Chaser to Nicky when he died."

"Oh!" Mike's brows shot up. "I think she mentioned something about that earlier."

Harry's horse and their saddle horse walked steadily beside Mike and Storm Chaser. Mike felt his chest expand, knowing he'd been given the honor of riding Nicky's horse.

Harry grinned. "Did she mention you're now riding a horse worth around one hundred thousand dollars?"

"What?" Mike spluttered and looked at the horse, suddenly nervous. "He's *that* expensive?"

"Yup!" Harry nodded. "I heard that Nicky's been offered nearly double that because he still has unbeaten racing records."

"Why isn't he racing anymore?" Mike asked.

"Nicky's father was the one that did the racing circuit," Harry told him. "Storm Chaser started when he was two years old and was only on the circuit for a year when Nicky's dad died." He shrugged. "He is just over five now, and most racehorses retire at five, but they'd take him for breeding purposes."

"Ah!" Mike nodded. "He has champion bloodlines."

"Exactly!" Harry nodded. "Are you comfortable speeding up a bit? We've fallen way behind."

"Sure!" Mike said, trying to look confident, but his heart started to race as he gently nudged the expensive horse into a trot beside Harry.

Nicky

The trail heading to Pan's Waterfall meandered through a lush forest, where the canopy of swaying palm fronds and subtropical trees provided dappled shade. The air was alive with the soothing sounds of birdsong and the occasional rustling of leaves as a gentle breeze swept through them. The earthy scent of damp soil and flora filled Nicky's senses, grounding her in the natural beauty of the landscape.

As horse and rider drew nearer to the waterfall, the soft murmur of running water grew louder, promising the hidden spectacle that lay ahead. The trail suddenly opened onto a small clearing, revealing Pan's Waterfall in all its glory.

The waterfall, framed by ancient moss-covered rocks, cascaded gracefully from a modest height into a crystal-clear pool below. Sunlight filtered through the surrounding foliage, creating a play of dancing light on the water's surface. The pool shimmered with inviting coolness, a tempting respite from the warmth of the Florida sun.

Large, mossy boulders, worn smooth by years of nature's caress, offered perfect resting spots for a picnic or just to sit and take in the breathtaking view. Tall grasses swayed in the gentle breeze at the water's edge, adding a touch of whimsy to the scene.

A rustic wooden picnic area was thoughtfully placed nearby, tempting visitors to linger and enjoy a meal amidst the serene ambiance where wooden benches and tables were scattered to provide comfortable seating.

The soft rush of the waterfall provided a soothing background melody as Nicky reined in Midnight, and they slowed to a trot. Pan's Waterfall always reminded Nicky of a place where time seemed to stand still. It was a haven for quiet reflection, a backdrop for cherished memories, and a testament to the unspoiled beauty of the natural world tucked away in the heart of Marco Island's outskirts.

Nicky sighed and filled her lungs with the fresh, cool air, leaning over to pat Midnight as they walked toward the water's edge. She walked him around the edge of the large sparkling pool, allowing the cool spray of the waterfall to sprinkle his coat.

"You need to cool down before I allow you to drink, beautiful boy," Nicky cooed as she slipped out of the saddle and pulled a brush out of the saddle bag.

Nicky took Midnight's saddle off and put it on one of the rocks surrounding the craggy waterfall. She allowed him to stand near the waterfall to feel the cool breeze but not too close as she took the brush and rubbed him down with it. His shiny black coat was wet with exertion, and his skin shuddered as she brushed him.

"I know you want to rush into Horses Pool, but you can't do that right now." Nicky laughed at him as he playfully nudged her as she stood in front of him to brush his neck. "Hey, quit it. You're going to push me into the Pan's Pond."

Midnight moved his neck up and down as if he was laughing.

"Cheeky!" Nicky kissed him just above his nose. "Come on, let's take you for a walk through Horses' Pond."

There were two sides to the Pan's Waterfall. As it fell down the rock, it split into two pools, and the larger one was where the animals were allowed to swim. Nicky took Midnight toward the pond. She kicked off her boots, pulled herself onto Midnight's back, and nudged him into the pond. Nicky didn't have to encourage Midnight too hard, either. The horse loved the water and waded in eagerly.

The pond had a smooth bottom with nothing hazardous for the horses and had been used for centuries to train the horses on the farm.

As Midnight waded further into the pond, the water gradually deepened, cooling his legs and belly. Nicky leaned forward, letting her fingers trail through the water, feeling its refreshing touch.

The sensation of riding Midnight through the water was exhilarating. The horse's powerful muscles rippled beneath her, and the splashing of his hooves created a symphony of liquid music. Nicky's heart danced to the rhythm of Midnight's movements as they glided through the pond.

The scenery around them was nothing short of magical. The sunlight filtered through the trees, casting dappled patterns on the water's surface. Dragonflies flitted about, their iridescent wings catching the sunlight. Overhead, a pair of ospreys circled, their sharp eyes searching for fish in the clear waters below.

As they ventured deeper into the pond, the water reached Midnight's chest, and Nicky could feel his enthusiasm. His powerful strokes propelled them forward, and soon, they reached the center of

Horses' Pond, where the water was at its deepest. Here, they paused for a moment, surrounded by the tranquility of nature.

Nicky closed her eyes, savoring the feeling of the water around them and the bond she shared with Midnight. It was a moment of pure connection, where words were unnecessary, and the beauty of the world enveloped them. With a gentle nudge of her heels, Nicky guided Midnight towards the shallower part of the pond. They continued their leisurely stroll through the water, cherishing the serenity of the place, knowing that moments like these were rare and precious.

Nicky loved animals, especially horses and dogs. It was a passion she had nurtured since childhood, spending countless hours at the Bailey's horse ranch on the outskirts of Marco Island. She had learned to ride there, forging a deep connection with the majestic creatures that roamed the ranch's pastures.

For Nicky, animals had become her silent confidants, offering solace in times of profound personal turmoil. The knowledge that she could never have children had left her with scars that ran deeper than mere words could express. The turmoil of her divorce and selling the home she'd so lovingly chosen in Miami had ripped her to the core.

Returning to Marco Island, surrounded by the serene beauty of nature, the comforting support of her family, and the companionship of horses like Storm and Midnight, was her way of finding healing. In the soft, knowing eyes of these animals, she discovered a unique kind of therapy. Their presence, their unspoken empathy, eased the ache in her heart. The rhythmic beat of hooves on the earth, the gentle nuzzle of a horse's muzzle, and the unwavering loyalty of her beloved basset hound, Belvedere, provided a sense of comfort and understanding that words could not.

In the company of these creatures, Nicky found a refuge where her soul could mend and the weight of her past could be momentarily lifted. They didn't ask questions, didn't judge her, or offer empty sympathy; instead, they just loved her with an unwavering innocence that transcended the complexities of human emotions.

With their gentle eyes and graceful movements, the horses understood her need for solace. They communicated in a language older than words, a silent understanding that ran deeper than the deepest wounds. Storm Chaser offered her his quiet strength and was her trusted steed. But Midnight, in particular, seemed to sense her pain and offered his back as a literal and metaphorical means of support. He, too, had something ripped from him when his racing career ended due to an injury, and they shared a pain no one else really understood.

Belvedere, her loyal basset hound, was a constant presence by her side, his mournful eyes replaced by a sense of purpose when they were together. His tail wagged with the simple joy of being in her company, a reminder that life could still hold moments of happiness, even in the midst of her struggles.

In their world, Nicky found solace and healing. The tranquility of the ranch, the soft rustle of leaves, and the earthy scent of hay and horsehair provided a sanctuary where she could breathe freely, away from the prying eyes and well-intentioned but often painful questions of friends and family. Here, Nicky didn't need to explain herself or justify her choices. She could simply exist, finding comfort in the company of these creatures who loved her unconditionally, reminding her that life was still beautiful in all its simplicity.

The sound of laughter intruded into her silence as she sat on the rocks in the sun, drying her riding pants, and Midnight grazed at the edges of the pond. As she looked up, her breath caught in her throat, surprising her. Mike looked a lot more relaxed upon Storm Chaser.

The comparison was impossible to ignore. Both man and horse were striking in their own right. Storm Chaser, the Akhal-Teke stallion, was a vision of elegance and power. His silver coat gleamed in the sunlight with a metallic sheen that made him appear almost otherworldly. His black face, adorned with a distinctive white diamond on his forehead, gave him an air of regal charm. His ears, mane, tail, and slender legs, all in silky black, contrasted beautifully with his radiant silver coat.

And then there was Mike. Tall, with a rugged handsomeness that seemed to belong to the wind and sea. His dark brown hair, kissed by the sun, framed a face that bore the lines of a life well-lived. His hazel eyes held a spark of humor as he laughed, creating crinkles at the corners. Dressed in jeans and a cotton shirt, he looked much more relaxed riding Storm Chaser.

Nicky shook herself mentally, suddenly self-conscious of her own appearance. She was damp from her earlier swim with Midnight, her riding pants and shirt clinging to her. As she continued to watch him, a smile tugged at the corners of her lips. He looked a lot more relaxed than he'd been the day before. But then, the Bailey's horse ranch seemed to have a way of unraveling the layers of stress and worry, revealing the person beneath.

Nicky felt her heart flutter, and she sucked in a breath to calm herself and put her weird feelings down to the magic of Pan's Waterfall, a tableau of tranquility and beauty that mirrored the harmony of nature. For a moment, the weight of her past and the uncertainty of her future seemed to fade into the background. Here, in the company of these majestic creatures, the beautiful scenery, fresh air, and good company, she found herself on the cusp of something new—she glanced at Mike and felt her heart lurch—and unexpected.

"Nicky!" Jade called as she walked her horse to where Nicky was standing up.

"Hi," Nicky greeted the teenager with a warm smile. "How are you and Arrow getting along?"

"I love Arrow," Jade told her, sliding out of the saddle and walking the horse toward them. "She's a great horse."

"But you have your heart set on Midnight." Nicky patted Midnight's neck as he lazily grazed and ignored the humans talking about him. "He's a beautiful horse." Her mind was filled with memories of a happier time. "I used to ride him all the time when I came to visit my parents."

"You two do seem to have a bond I haven't seen with anyone else who rides him," Jade commented.

"We understand each other," Nicky's voice was soft, and she laughed when Midnight gave her a gentle nudge. "To be honest with you, I know my sisters say they want to sell him, but I doubt whether Steph will let them."

"Oh!" Jade's face fell, and she sighed.

"Don't feel blue," Nicky told her. "You are a great rider, but you still have a lot to learn, and your uncle is right to be concerned about you riding a horse like Midnight." She leaned forward and stroked Arrow. "I've seen how you and Arrow work together, and if you want to buy a horse, you should look at her." She laughed when Arrow whinnied and rubbed her nose on Nicky's arm. "She's a mustang with a beautiful spirit, just like you."

"She does," Jade agreed, looking conflicted as she looked from Midnight to Arrow. "It's just I feel like Midnight and I share a connection." Her voice dropped. "We both have broken souls."

Nicky's heart lurched at the young girl's words and the haunted look in her eyes.

"I felt like that too when we first got Midnight," Nicky told her, swallowing the burning lump rising in her throat. It was just after her second miscarriage. "He'd just recovered from an injury that ended his racing career, and I'd just recovered from one myself."

"Oh no," Jade looked at Nicky with compassion shining in her eyes. "I'm sorry."

"It's okay," Nicky assured her. "My sister told me about your parents." She gave Jade's arm a gentle squeeze. "That's another reason Arrow is the perfect fit for you."

"Why?" Jade's brow crumpled curiously.

"Arrow was a wild mustang who lost her parents when she was one year old," Nicky told her. "My older sister, Lorry, and I were visiting my mother's cousin in Montana when we found Arrow."

"You were the ones that saved her?" Jade's eyes widened.

"Yes," Nicky said, nodding and gently stroking Arrow's forehead. "But we got her to trust us, and she's been with us ever since."

"Won't it make you sad to sell her?" Jade asked, and Nicky saw she was slowly moving Jade toward buying Arrow.

"She's hardly ridden anymore, and Lorry and I won't let her go to just anyone," Nicky assured Jade.

"Are you trying to sell my niece a horse?" Mike's deep voice rang in Nicky's ears, making her jump and turn to look at him.

"Nicky's trying to talk me out of wanting to buy Midnight," Jade told him. "She feels Arrow is more suited to me."

"I have to agree with Nicky," Mike said. "Arrow is a beautiful horse. I watched you riding her. The two of you have a connection. It was like watching a well-harmonized symphony."

"Wow!" Jade's brows rose high on her forehead as she stared at her uncle. "Five minutes owning a bookstore, and you're talking like a poet." She laughed and hugged Mike. "You're so cheesy, Uncle Mike." She looked at Nicky. "Thanks, Nicky. I'm going to think about our talk." She looked at Arrow. "Would you mind if I rode her for the summer?"

"Not at all," Nicky told her. "Maybe we can meet once or twice a week and ride together."

"I'd like that," Jade said excitedly.

"That's if it's okay with your uncle." Nicky looked questioningly at Mike.

"I don't mind." Mike looked at her, amazed. "Thank you."

"I love riding." Nicky shrugged. "I come here as often as possible, and if Jade's free, I don't mind bringing her with me if she wants to ride."

"Yes, thank you, thank you," Jade squealed in delight and threw her arms around Nicky. "I'd love to."

With that, Jade led Arrow off to tell Gemma the exciting news.

"You do know that if you bring Jade, you'll probably have to bring Sam's kids as well?" Mike warned her.

"I don't mind." Nicky grinned. She loved kids, and maybe being around a bunch of teenagers on horses was precisely what she needed to help her heal. "How did you enjoy your ride on Storm Chaser?"

"Wow!" Mike said with a low whistle. "He is great."

"I know. Storm can be as gentle as a soft spring breeze, but don't let that fool you," Nicky warned him. "He can be even more temperamental than Midnight."

"I bet!" Mike ran his hand through his hair. "I was sent here to bring you to the picnic area for something to eat." His eyes ran the length of her. "Are you wet?"

"Yes, Midnight and I went for a swim in Horses Pond." Nicky laughed at the look of surprise on his face. "Midnight loves to swim."

"Thank you for talking my niece out of wanting to buy Midnight," Mike said. "It was better coming from you than me. I'm just the worried parent figure. But you're this experienced horse whisperer who is an amazing rider with a horse woven from silver thread."

Nicky's heart fluttered, and her throat went dry as his words seeped through the ice in her veins and started to warm her cold heart. She gave herself a mental shake and hoped she wasn't gaping at him as she gathered her composure.

"Thank you!" Nicky cleared her throat. "Shall we go eat? I'm starved." She changed the subject.

Before he could answer, Nicky nearly knocked Mike out of the way as she made a nervous beeline to the table where Harry and Sam had set out the picnic. Her heart was hammering wildly in her chest, and she felt all tingly from his compliment—a feeling she hadn't felt in many years.

CHAPTER 7

M ike was finishing the inventory at Sully's Corner while his mind wandered back to when he and Jade had gone horse riding a few days ago. It had been an unexpectedly enjoyable day at the Bailey's horse ranch. They had gone there for a trail ride with his niece and Harry's family to find a horse to buy Jade. But they were joined by four of the Scott sisters, including Nicky, and the day had turned into a picnic at Pan's Waterfall.

Mike sighed as he pictured Nicky perched on top of her ethereal horse. Their combined beauty had taken his breath away. Nicky was skilled on horseback, and Jade had taken an immediate liking to her. While he was a little self-conscious being a new rider around Nicky, he'd soon relaxed as she never once teased him or judged him on being so green when it came to horseback riding. Mike had also made a mental note to send her a bouquet to thank her for talking Jade out of wanting to buy Midnight and set her sights on Arrow instead.

It was such a relief when Jade told Mike she would prefer Arrow as her Christmas gift on the way home from Bailey's Ranch. Then, for the rest of the day, Jade couldn't stop talking about Nicky and all the tips she'd given Jade about riding. The two of them planned to meet on Wednesday. Mike's heart lurched at the thought of seeing Nicky again when she came to fetch Jade. He gave his head a shake.

"Good grief, I'm acting like a schoolboy with a crush," Mike muttered as the soft jingle of the store's front doorbell caught his attention.

He snorted as his heart once again skipped a beat at the thought it might be Nicky coming to discuss her offer for the bookstore. He took a steadying breath and forced himself not to rush to the door. But when he reached the front, his heart sank as he saw Mandy Oliver, a local real estate agent, waving at him through the glass.

I really need to get a blind to cover this door. Mike sighed and glanced at the window to see the for sale sign was still there.

"Hi, Mandy." Mike welcomed her inside.

"Hello Mike," Mandy greeted, stepping into the store, and they exchanged pleasantries.

"I hope you didn't come to buy a book," Mike joked, knowing it was more likely Mandy came to visit because of the sign in the window. "Because I'm not open for business right now."

Mandy grinned and replied, "No, I'm not much of a reader," she admitted. "I prefer to wait for the movies to come out."

"Some of my friends are like that, too." Mike laughed.

"I'm here to do an assessment of the store for Nicky. She's quite interested in purchasing it," Mandy told him. "I know she's already made you an offer, but I want to assess it anyway.|

Mike nodded, though his uncertainty about selling the store was evident. "Ah, yes. I've been considering the offer, but I must admit I'm not entirely sure if I want to part with my late uncle's legacy." He sighed. "I think I was too hasty to put up that for sale sign after Jade and I first got here a few weeks ago."

Understanding his hesitation, Mandy leaned forward slightly, her tone sympathetic. "I understand, Mike. It's never easy to let go of something with such sentimental value. But from a business perspective, Nicky is the right person to ensure Sully's legacy is well taken care of." She shook her head. "You could always find Nicky in here when we were young."

"I know." Mike glanced around the cozy bookstore, his fingers tracing the edge of an old bookshelf. "You may be right about Nicky, but it's still a difficult decision for me."

Mandy nodded, her eyes fixed on Mike. "I can appreciate that. It's a big step. That's why I'm here to help you determine the store's value and provide guidance."

Mike gestured toward the rows of books. "Well, go ahead and take a look. I'm curious to know what it's worth."

Mandy appreciated his willingness to cooperate and began her assessment. After a thorough examination, she joined Mike at the front of the store.

"Mike, I have to be honest. Nicky's offer is more than fair. In fact, it exceeds the market value of the store." Mandy looked around, her eyes falling on the double doors that led to the back balcony that overlooked the beach. "The building needs quite a bit of work." She nodded toward the sea. "But the store's location is its biggest worth at the moment."

"Yes, that and Sully's rare book collection," Mike told her and noted her head snap toward him, her eyes wide with interest.

"Sully has a rare book collection?" Mandy looked at him in surprise.

"Yes, but it's not part of the shop's inventory." Mike glanced toward the sea as memories of his uncle flashed before him, squeezing at his heart before he looked at Mandy again. "It's his own private collection."

"Pity." Mandy pulled a face. "That would increase the store's price and make it more attractive to other potential buyers should you not accept Nicky's offer." She walked to the counter where Mike was standing. "But honestly, I advise you to seriously consider Nicky's offer. It's probably the best you'll get for this place." She raised her brows. "Nicky will run it as a bookstore while other parties interested in it would be development companies as this is a prime spot for the tourist trade."

"Great. That's just what we need—more malls." Mike shook his head and blew out a breath, his brows furrowed as he was torn by the decision. He ran a hand through his hair as he held Mandy's eyes. "I appreciate your input. It's just that this place holds so many memories."

Mandy placed a reassuring hand on his shoulder. "I know it's not easy, but sometimes, life takes unexpected turns. If you decide to sell to Nicky, you'll ensure that Sully's Corner continues to thrive." She pursed her lips. "If you wait to sell, you could lose Nicky's interest in the property and open the door for a development firm."

Mike nodded slowly, processing her words. "I suppose you're right. I just need some time to think it over."

Mandy smiled, understanding his reluctance. "Of course. But remember, Nicky is the best person to entrust this place to."

Mike contemplated her advice for a moment. "I know Nicky is waiting for an answer. I just can't decide." He shook his head. "I'm sure that out of everyone on the planet, my uncle would love for the new owner of his store to be Nicky."

Mandy's face lit up with a smile, and he could see an idea forming in her mind. "Why don't you consider letting Nicky buy into the store." She glanced around again. "That way, you're not losing it entirely but taking on a business partner. That will give you a cash injection to renovate, modernize, and get the store up and running."

Mike's eyes brightened at the suggestion. "That sounds like a good idea." His mind started clicking over with possibilities.

"You could run the store together for a few months." Mandy's eyes reflected her thoughts. "That will also give you more time to decide if you want to sell it." She grinned. "It will also keep big development companies from swooping in and turning this beautiful part of our town into a tourist trap."

"You don't like big development companies much, do you?" Mike laughed at the look Mandy shot him. "That's strange for a real estate agent."

"I'm a real estate agent with a conscience who wants to preserve my heritage and keep the natural beauty of our coastline," Mandy's voice was filled with contempt. She pulled a business card from her purse and handed it to Mike. "Here is my card. Let me know what you decided, and if you want to look into a partnership for a couple of months, I'll set that up with Nicky."

"Thank you," Mike told her, taking the card. "I think that's an intriguing offer. Just give me a day or two to think it over." He looked at Mandy's business card. "Have you taken over your parent's real estate business?"

"I have," Mandy told him as she headed toward the front door. "They've retired and headed to their condo in Tampa."

"Nice." Mike smiled as he opened the door for her. "I'm glad you took over their company, and it's good to know you hold the same property values that your parents did."

"Of course." Mandy laughed, stepping through the door. "I completely agree with their policies about there being a place for malls, hotels, and unobstructed views of our country's natural beauty." She glanced at her wristwatch. "Goodness, I have to run." She looked at Mike. "It was good to see you again, Mike, and I'll wait to hear from you. I'll let Nicky know you'll get back to us in the next few days."

"Does Nicky know about your joint ownership idea?" Mike asked.

"No." Mandy shook her head. "I came up with that when I told you about it." She gave him a reassuring smile. "Don't worry. I'll talk to Nicky about it when we meet for lunch today, and I'm positive she'll like the idea."

"Thank you, Mandy." Mike waved her off as she walked toward her car parked on the curb in front of the bookstore.

As he closed and locked the door, Mike's eyes dropped to the business card. A feeling of excitement coursed through him at the idea of jointly owning the bookstore with Nicky. Not only would it keep the bookstore in his family, but he'd get to work with her and see her often. While he could deny it all he wanted to Harry, Mike knew the truth was that he'd been in love with Nicky Scott since they were in high school.

Mike insisted on spending summer vacation with his uncle so he could work in the bookstore, knowing that Nicky was there nearly every day. When she wasn't in the store, he knew he could probably find her sitting in her favorite spot on the beach in front of the Scott family's home and hotel. Which was conveniently just up the road from the store and Mike's uncle's cottage. Mike had never been shy around women and didn't have a problem dating until it came to Nicky—he could never pluck up the courage to ask her out.

Mike stood staring out the double glass doors at the ocean beyond them, idly tapping the business card in his hand. A smile spread across his face, and lifted the card. His heart skipped a beat as he pulled out his phone. Mike didn't need two days to decide about Mandy's idea. Why put off for two days what he already knew he would do.

Mike typed Mandy's number into his phone and hit the dial button. She answered after the fourth ring.

"Mike?" Mandy sounded surprised. "Have you come to a decision already?"

"I have," Mike told her and frowned. "How did you know it was me?"

"I have your number programmed into my phone from the for sale sign in the bookstore's window," Mandy told him. "What did you decide?" She asked. "Am I delivering bad or potentially good news to Nicky at lunchtime?"

"If Nicky is willing to become a joint owner for a couple of months, I'll certainly be more willing to sell the bookstore to her after three months." Mike watched the sparkling blue ocean meander lazily past the shore.

"Great!" Mandy said. "I'll speak to Nicky and get back to you. If she agrees, we can all sit down together and go over the details."

"Thank you, Mandy," Mike told her with a smile splitting his face as his heart and soul felt lighter. "I think this will make it much easier for me to finally sell the store."

"You're going ahead with the sale?" Harry's voice came from behind Mike, making him spin around in fright.

"Geez, Mike, don't sneak up on me like that!" Mike moaned.

"I didn't sneak up on you." Harry frowned. "I called when I walked into the store, but you were on the phone."

"I was speaking to Mandy Oliver," Mike told him.

"You've given her the listing?" Harry's brow furrowed tighter.

"Sort of!" Mike said, scrunching up his face.

"What does sort of mean when it comes to selling the bookstore?" Harry persisted.

"Mandy came to see me to assess the shop for Nicky," Mike explained. "She noticed that I was reluctant to sell the store, and she came up with a great plan."

"Okay!" Harry looked at him questioningly.

"She suggested that I let Nicky buy into the store as a partner for three months," Mike told Harry about the plan. "Nicky and I run the store together and return it to a fully operational business. Then I can decide after three months if I want to sell it to Nicky or continue our partnership."

"And Nicky's on board with this idea?" Harry looked skeptical. "Because the offer she gave you the other day seemed like she wanted to buy the store outright."

"Mandy's going to pitch the idea to Nicky today over lunch." Mike slipped Mandy's business card into a drawer behind the sales counter.

"That sounds like a great idea for you," Harry pointed out. "But don't be too disappointed if Nicky doesn't go for it."

"I won't," Mike lied and glanced around the store. "You were right the other day." He sighed. "I'm not ready to let go of this place. It holds too many memories of Uncle Sully, my childhood with my brother, and it's also part of Jade's legacy."

"And if Nicky goes for the idea, it'll become only part of yours and Jade's legacy," Harry told him.

"I'm fine with that," Mike assured Harry.

"What about Jade?" Harry asked. "Sam asked Jade the other day how she felt about you selling Sully's Corner, and she was quite sad about it."

"Oh!" Mike's eyes widened as he realized he hadn't even asked Jade how she felt about selling the place. "I didn't even ask her."

"That's because you're still a bachelor at heart," Harry teased him. "I think Jade will be okay with whatever you decide as long as you keep the cottage because she loves it here on the island."

"I know." Mike nodded. "She's convinced me to look into buying Arrow from the Scotts for her."

"Ah, so you are going to get her a horse?" Harry enquired.

"You saw how good she is with horses and how well she rides," Mike told him. "I can't deny her something that brings her so much joy."

"Or how much closer it will bring you to a certain Nicky Scott?" Harry teased.

"What is wrong with you?" Mike shook his head at his friend. "Nicky is just someone who wants to buy the store and enjoys the company of people who are interested in horses like she is."

"I hope you like bassetts as much as you've started to like horses." Harry grinned.

"What are you talking about?" Mike frowned.

"Jade offered to walk Nicky's basset for her." Mike pointed through the back doors. "Unless you got a dog in the last twenty-four hours. I'm pretty sure that's Nicky's dog."

"What?" Mike said and spun around to see Jade and Harry's daughter Gemma running toward the bookstore from the beach with a basset hound. "How do you know more than I do about my niece?"

"I live in a house that is currently mostly female, and your niece is there with Gemma nearly every day." Harry shrugged. "I hear things."

"Well, thanks for the heads up about the dog," Mike hissed.

"Ah!" Harry nodded in understanding. "You're still not good with them, then?"

"It's not me!" Mike defended himself. "It's them. Dogs just don't like me."

"Nor do cats." Harry reminded him. "Oh..." He grinned. "And parrots. Do you remember Pirate Pete, Sully's parrot?" He gave a low whistle and shook his head. "That bird and you did not get along."

"Pirate Pete was a very large Macaw with a bad attitude!" Mike looked at Harry wide-eyed. "He was jealous of my relationship with my uncle."

"He was fine with everyone else," Harry pointed out. "And I mean *everyone* else."

"Can we not talk about that horrid bird." Mike suppressed a shudder, remembering his late uncle's parrot.

"Uncle Angus had a parrot?" Jade asked, she and Gemma catching the back end of the conversation as they rushed into the bookstore with the large floppy-eared dog.

"Yes, he did," Harry answered before Mike could. "Your Uncle Mike had nightmares that Pirate Pete would outlive Sully, and as Mike was his only heir, he was afraid he'd have to take on the care of the bird."

"Oh, no!" Jade looked at Harry. "Is it even birds that don't get along with Uncle Mike?"

"Uh-huh!" Harry nodded.

"I'm standing right here!" Mike reminded them. "And I get along with animals."

To prove his point, Mike leaned down to pat Belvedere, who, to everyone's surprise, flopped over onto his bag and acted like a possum.

"Wow!" Harry exclaimed. "The dog's acting dead to avoid you."

Harry, Jade, and Gemma laughed as Mike crouched down and scratched the basset's stomach.

"See, he wanted me to scratch his tummy," Mike said, proud of his accomplishment.

"This is Belvedere, Uncle Mike. He's Nicky's dog," Gemma told him. "Jade and I volunteered to walk him for her a few times a week."

"He's wonderful." Jade kneeled beside her uncle. "Hey, boy. You like my Uncle Mike just fine, don't you?"

Belvedere gave an appreciative moan for all the attention and belly rubs he was getting.

"He is cute," Mike said, standing up. "But no, you're not getting a dog."

"Oh, come on, Uncle Mike!" Jade's brow crumpled.

"It's either a horse or a dog," Mike gave her a choice. "Not both."

"Fine," Jade stood, and Belvedere flopped onto his belly, lying at Jade's feet. "I'll take Arrow."

"That's settled then," Mike said before he realized how neatly he'd been manipulated.

"Really?" Jade's eyes lit with excitement. She and Gemma squealed in delight, and Jade wrapped her arms around Mike. "Thank you, thank you."

"Well played, young grasshopper." Harry grinned as he eyed Jade. "Well played. You really are your mother's daughter. She, too, knew just how to play her older brother."

"Hey!" Mike exclaimed again. "I'm right here."

"Wasn't there something you wanted to discuss with Jade?" Harry asked Mike. He took the leash from Jade's hand. "Myself and Gemma will finish Belvedere's walk and let the two of you talk." He ushered his daughter and Belvedere from the store before Mike could protest. "Come on, Gem."

"What do you want to talk to me about, Uncle Mike?" Jade looked at him curiously. "Is it about Arrow?"

"No, honey," Mike said with a shake of his head. "This is about the bookstore."

"Oh!" Jade looked relieved. "What about it?"

"I should've spoken to you before I put it up for sale," Mike admitted. "It's part of your legacy as well, and I never asked you what you wanted to do with the place."

Jade smiled. "Honestly, I don't want you to sell it," she admitted. "But I understand that we live in Miami, and it would be difficult to try and run the business from there ."

"What if we stayed on Marco Island for the rest of the summer and see how we feel about maybe moving here for good?" Mike had no idea why he'd suggested that, as the idea had just popped into his head, and it felt right.

"Really?" Jade's eyes widened and sparkled with delight. "You'd consider moving here for good?" Her smile broadened. "I could go to school here with Gemma? I'd love that."

"So would I." Mike smiled as he realized just how much he meant it.

He wrapped his arms around Jade when she flung herself at him joyfully.

"What about the store?" Jade stepped away from him. "Nicky's going to be devastated when you tell her it's no longer for sale."

"About that..." Mike's words trailed off. "This place still needs a lot of work and someone who has experience in how to run the place."

"You know how to do that," Jade said.

"No, honey." Mike laughed at her enthusiasm and faith in him. "I need help because I still have my career. Even though I can work from anywhere, it will take up the best part of my day like usual."

"Oh!" Jade's face fell. "So you're still going to sell the bookshop."

"No, Mandy Oliver, a real estate agent, came to see me today and made a great suggestion," Mike said with a grin. "How would you feel about us getting a partner for the bookstore?"

"It's a huge yes if by a partner you mean Nicky," Jade told him, her grin resurfacing.

"No promises because Mandy still has to run the idea past Nicky, but yes, I was thinking of offering half of the business to Nicky," Mike told her, a variant of Mandy's proposal. He'd somehow find a way around that three-month clause, but that was a problem for another day.

"I'm sure Nicky will say yes," Jade's enthusiasm spilled into her voice and shone in her eyes. She gave Mike another hug. "This is the best day ever." She stated. "I get to walk Belvedere, we're moving to Marco Island, and I'm getting Arrow." She kissed Mike on the cheek. "Can I tell Gemma?"

"Can you rather ask Harry and Gemma to come back, and we tell them together?" Mike suggested.

"Okay!" Jade was out the door before he could stop.

She'd no sooner when his phone rang, and he saw it was Mandy. His heart did a flip.

"Hi, Mandy," Mike greeted her.

"Hey, Mike," Mandy greeted him back. "I have news."

"Okay," Mike said, holding his breath as his heartbeat accelerated.

"Nicky agreed to your terms of a three-month trial partnership," Mandy told him excitedly. "She asked if you could meet us tomorrow at my office."

"Sure, what time?" Mike asked, clearing his throat, realizing he sounded breathless.

CHAPTER 8

Nicky sat on the deck of Scott House, savoring the deep red hues painted across the sky as the sun dipped below the horizon. She was in the company of her sisters, Lorry and Steph, who stared at her in surprise after hearing her news about investing in the bookstore two days ago.

Stephanie, the younger of the two, broke the silence, her voice laced with awe. "Wow, Nicky."

Lorry, the more cautious of the sisters, expressed her concern. "Are you sure it's a good idea? Aren't you stretching yourself thin financially, especially with all your recent investments?" She swirled the red wine in her glass. "Not to mention the trust you set up to help

Megan Riley with her tuition fees for med school, and you're looking at buying Riley Cottage from her."

Nicky waved away Lorry's worry, explaining, "I won't be paying the full amount upfront, and I'm genuinely excited about running a bookstore." Excitement bubbled within her, and she continued, "You know, I've always dreamed of owning Sully's Corner."

"Okay then." Lorry raised her glass, offering a supportive toast, and they all chimed in, "To dreams coming true."

"Where is Mom?" Steph asked, glancing towards the glass door. "She's been going out a lot lately."

Nicky shared the recent changes in their mother's behavior. "She's been spending more time with friends from the tennis club."

"Maybe she's got a secret boyfriend?" Steph speculated.

Lorry, doubtful, interjected, "I doubt that. Dad was the love of her life."

Changing the subject, Nicky turned her attention to Lorry, "What about you, Lorry? Isn't it time to move on from your divorce?"

Steph joined in, "It's been seven years, Lorry."

Lorry sighed, admitting, "You're both right. But you know I've dedicated my life to my daughter, our family, and the hotel."

Nicky, concerned for her sister's happiness, encouraged, "You need to take some time for yourself and find someone you deserve."

"I've been telling her that since her divorce," Steph told Nicky before looking at Lorry.

The conversation shifted to their father, and the sisters contemplated the mysterious bank account he had maintained. Nicky was suspicious, given her own experiences.

"You don't think dad had another family, do you?" Lorry's brow was knit tightly together as she looked from Nicky to Steph.

Steph remained skeptical. "No way!" She shook her head emphatically. "There must be another explanation."

"I still think it was just so weird how Mom swooped in and stopped us from trying to discover why Dad had set up that account," Lorry said, chewing the side of her mouth thoughtfully.

"You said Mom got angry when you and Steph tried to push the matter." Nicky looked at Lorry.

"Oh, yes." Lorry's eyebrows shot up as she pulled a face and blew out a breath. "I've never seen her so angry."

"Does she know that you've stopped payments to the account?" Nicky looked at her two sisters worriedly.

"No!" Steph answered. "Luckily, Dad left Lorry in charge of all money matters."

"The only account I didn't have control of was that mysterious one that Mom wouldn't let us dig into," Lorry continued the story from

Steph. "So I shut down all the old accounts once we were able to pay off the loans eight months ago and opened new ones for the businesses."

"Businesses?" Nicky's eyes narrowed.

"Yes, Dad owns half of Bailey's Horse Ranch and stables," Steph surprised her by saying. "We found out that the Bailey's were in financial trouble, and Dad bailed them out by investing in the ranch."

"That's why they're not charging me a stabling fee," Nicky said and then looked at Lorry. "Then why are you selling some of our horses?"

"I was only selling Midnight, Arrow, and Ghost," Lorry told her. "I feel bad that they are not getting ridden as often as they should be."

"I'm here now," Nicky said. "And I love those horses." She looked pleadingly at Lorry. "Please don't sell them. I'll pay all their costs."

"Yes, and I love Midnight," Stephanie protested. "Dad said he was all of ours to share."

"You don't ride him enough, Steph." Lorry turned her attention to Steph before looking at Nicky. "Yes, the costs are a major concern," she admitted. "But we don't get to ride as often as we used to."

"Yes, but I'm here now, and you know I ride *at least* three times a week," Nicky reminded them. "Even more some weeks when I can slip away."

"Okay, I'll think about it," Lorry promised, giving Nicky a patient smile. "How are you going to exercise all our horses?" She shook her head. "With Storm Chaser back at the stables we currently have nine horses there."

"Are you still letting some of them be used for trail rides?" Nicky asked.

"Only three of them," Steph told her. "Arrow, Mischa, and Tomboy."

"Ghost, Trident, Ripple, Pegasus, and Whisper don't like just anyone riding them," Lorry pointed out.

"You mean none of you like your horses being ridden by strangers." Nicky laughed. "I don't blame you. So, no judgment. I'd hate for anyone to ride Storm Chaser." Her brow furrowed as she realized they hadn't mentioned Dancer. "I meant to ask you a few days ago where Dancer was."

Nicky didn't miss the look her sisters exchanged.

"What happened to Dancer?" Nicky looked accusingly at her sisters before her eyes widened. "Did you sell her?"

Dancer had been Lorry's horse. Ghost had been Nicky's. When their father died, he'd left Storm Chaser to Nicky. Lorry had always loved Ghost, so Nicky had given Ghost to her, and Lorry had given Dancer to her daughter, Tammy, a year ago.

"No!" Stephanie was quick to answer.

"I thought you gave her to Tammy," Nicky looked at Lorry. "You said she was interested in riding again about a year ago."

"As you know, my daughter still blames me for the divorce," Lorry explained, her eyes dropping to her wine to hide the hurt that always flashed in them when she spoke about Tammy. She blew out a breath, and her hand shook slightly when she lifted the glass to her lips.

"I thought Tammy really wanted Dancer?" Nicky's frown deepened.

"I love Tammy." Steph's eyes widened as she spoke, and she gestured with her hand. "You'd think after seven years she'd finally see through her father and that the divorce was entirely his fault."

"Steph!" Lorry looked at her warningly.

"No, Lorry, I'm sorry, but Tammy is getting worse," Steph stated, looking at Nicky. "Tammy *rented* out Dancer to a movie company filming a western in Naples."

"She did what?" Nicky looked at her sisters in disbelief.

Lorry sighed, closed her eyes, and gave her head a slight shake before looking at Nicky. "A month ago, she brought me some legal documents to sign stating that Dancer was her horse," Lorry explained to Nicky. "I thought it was Tammy's way of proving to me she was becoming more responsible, so I'd finally let her take the shuttle on her own to visit her father when she wanted to."

119

"But *no*," Steph emphasized the no, her eyes blazing, which was uncharacteristic of her usually cool, calm, and soft sister. "Little Miss Tammy was plotting ways to make money so she wouldn't have to ask Lorry for any so she could leave before dawn to go to Naples and visit her father."

"Tammy did that?" Nicky gasped. "You said about a month ago?" She looked at Lorry, confused. "Why am I only hearing about this now?"

"Shh," Lorry said, putting her index finger to her lips. "Mom and Gran don't know what Tammy did, and I don't want them to."

"Lorry!" Nicky admonished. "I've seen and known Tammy to pull some stunts, but that's not only hurtful to you, it's also dangerous for a young girl to sneak off like that."

"She is sixteen," Lorry defended her daughter. "We're in Florida, so she can legally drop out of school if she wants to and become independent."

"Yes, but only with *your* signed consent," Steph reminded Lorry.

"Can we not do this, please?" Lorry looked stressed. "I know Tammy is becoming more of a handful, but Grant and his new young wife are expecting their first baby."

"Which means Grant already has his next new wife lined up!" Steph hissed.

"Steph!" Lorry said, exasperated.

"I agree with Steph," Nicky said. "I know I have no room to talk here, but Grant was a complete womanizer, and the moment he found out you were pregnant with Tammy, he started playing the field."

"He was a jerk," Lorry admitted. "But that jerk is also my daughter's father."

"And you've defended him to Tammy her whole life," Steph pointed out.

"Yes, yes." Lorry sighed. "I've no one to blame for my daughter's terrible attitude toward me but myself."

"No, Lorry." Nicky reached over and squeezed her sister's hand. "All you're guilty of is being a great mom." She gave her an encouraging smile. "You didn't want your and Grant's problems to become Tammy's in order for her to have a good relationship with her father."

"Which proves that you were always way too good for Grant Chandler," Steph said.

"Thank you, my sisters." Lorry laughed before taking another sip of her wine. "I do miss my little troublemaker."

"When does she return from Grant's place?" Nicky asked.

"In a week," Lorry answered, moving the subject away from her daughter. "We still need to find out about Dad's secret account."

"I don't think it's because he had a second family," Steph said. "There has to be another explanation."

"Steph, honey, having been through it," Nicky said, "I think I know the signs now, and a mysterious bank account where Dad deposited a *large sum* of money every six months is suspicious."

"Yes, but it could've been anything," Steph defended their late father's honor.

"I have to go with Nicky on this one, Steph," Lorry looked at their younger sister. "You don't see the signs because you were lucky enough to get a one-in-a-billion guy." She smiled. "And you have every mother's dream teenage twin boys that don't give you a moment's trouble."

"Yes, sister dearest, you have the perfect marriage and family," Nicky agreed with Lorry. "I must admit we're all very happy for you but also a little jealous." She laughed.

"Yes, I'm lucky." Steph glanced toward the sea, but not before Nicky saw something worrying flash in her eyes. But when she looked their way again, it was gone. "But I've seen what the two of you have gone through, and I'm pretty sure I'd see the signs too." She sipped her iced tea. "Trust me, I'd have known if there was something like that going on with Dad."

"We want to believe that too," Lorry said. "But what I haven't told any of you yet is that it wasn't only a large lump sum every six months. Dad paid a smaller amount that would also equate to day-to-day living expenses each month to that account."

"What?" Nicky and Steph spluttered in unison.

"I wish we could find out more about that account," Lorry said, staring at the ocean. "But, it's no longer our concern now that I've moved the bank accounts, and we've managed to save the house and the hotel."

"And keep our shares in Bailey's Ranch," Steph added, beaming at Nicky. "All thanks to you, Nicky."

"It's my pleasure." Nicky raised her glass. "You should've come to me sooner, though." She smiled and then frowned at Steph's glass. "Steph, since I've been home, you haven't touched a drop of wine."

"She's on this weird diet!" Lorry answered for Steph.

"Why do you need to diet?" Nicky's eyes widened in disbelief.

"It's more a detoxing, resetting my system, type diet." Steph waved it off. "We all should be doing something to prepare our bodies for the next stage of our life."

There was that look in Steph's eyes again, Nicky noted.

"Is everything okay, Steph?" Nicky asked.

"Yes!" Steph frowned. "Why do you ask?"

"You love your wine but have changed it for herbal iced tea. You're not riding as much as you usually do." Nicky listed the things she'd noticed Steph had changed. "You've started power walking instead of jogging, and since I've been home, I've barely seen Max." Her eyes narrowed.

"You know my husband." Steph laughed, trying to make light of it. "He's been so busy at the Marine Center with the extension that I've hardly seen him. Thank you for asking and caring, but we're fine."

Nicky wasn't sure if Steph was trying to convince them or herself of that statement, and she could sense something wasn't right with her. Steph and her husband did everything together when they weren't at work. Even during their girl's nights, Max made a point of dropping Steph off and greeting everyone. He hadn't done that the past two times they'd had their weekly sisters' dinner night. Nicky couldn't remember seeing them hold hands or do their usual unabashed public displays of affection they were well known for.

Alarm spread through Nicky as she eyed her younger sister worriedly, hoping it was just her imagination and there was nothing wrong with Steph's marriage. She really had married the perfect guy, and Nicky wasn't lying when she'd told Steph the other five Scott sisters envied her. Nicky shook it off, putting her feelings down to paranoia after having her marriage blow up and the mystery of who their father was secretly paying money to.

"Nicky!" Jade's voice called from the beach as she came into view.

Nicky's heart lurched when she saw Jade running toward them with Belvedere, whom she'd taken for the afternoon, followed by Mike.

"So that's where Belvedere was!" Steph grinned as they watched the trio draw closer.

"Hi," Mike greeted them as he, Jade, and Belvedere stopped at the end of the deck. "Sorry to intrude on your evening, but we brought Belvedere home."

"Thank you for letting me look after him today," Jade said, walking onto the deck with Belvedere traipsing alongside her.

"You're welcome," Nicky said, pushing herself up and hoping her shaky legs would hold her.

"Hi, Jade," Steph and Lorry greeted the young girl before turning toward Mike. "Hi, Mike."

"Hi, ladies," Mike greeted them in unison with his niece.

"Would you like to join us for a glass of wine?" Steph invited him and then turned to Lorry. "We have an assortment of sodas and healthy iced teas."

"Oh, no, we don't want to disturb you," Mike told them.

"You won't be," Lorry assured him, giving Nicky a knowing look.

"I don't mind, Uncle Mike," Jade said.

"Okay." Mike nodded, stepping onto the deck.

"I'll get the wine," Lorry offered.

"Why don't I take Jade to choose a soda?" Steph stood at the same time Lorry did.

Before Nicky could say anything, the three of them and Belvedere disappeared into the house. She stood staring after them, her heart hammering against her ribs before turning toward Mike, who was always staring after the trio.

"Take a seat," Nicky told him.

"Thanks," Mike said and sat beside her. "This is a lovely deck."

"Yes, we like to sit out here in the evening and have sundowners," Nicky said and wanted to kick herself for stating the obvious.

"If it wasn't for the footpath that ran past the store, Riley Cottage, and my cottage, I'd like to put a deck out in front of my cottage like this," Mike told her.

"You could," Nicky said. "Extend the footpath toward the beach, and then you could put one long deck out for your and Megan's cottage and extend the store's deck."

"That's a good idea," Mike said, his brow furrowing thoughtfully. "I'm going to ask Tom to take a look at it and see if he can work his architect magic."

"Soon, you'll be having sundowners on a deck, too," Nicky said with a grin. "I love curling up with a book on a lounger in the morning sun."

"That explains your sun-kissed skin," Mike told her, making her heart go wild and her cheeks heat.

"You've also got a good tan," Nicky complimented him. Her eyes fell on the dark blue T-shirt stretched over his well-defined chest, and she gave herself a mental shake.

"It's a T-shirt tan," Mike confided with a grin. "I haven't tanned or taken my shirt off in the sun in about ten years." He gave a soft laugh. "While my arms and legs are tanned, trust me, my torso looks like a ghost."

"I have to admit to the same." Nicky grinned back. "Only I can wear strappy sundresses, so at least my shoulders and part of the back get tanned."

"Ah, the joys of being able to wear sundresses," Mike sighed exaggeratedly.

Their conversation about nothing was interrupted by an excited Jade as she rushed onto the deck with Belvedere trotting behind her.

"Uncle Mike, Gemma, and Aunt Sam have invited me to go to the movies with them." Jade showed him her phone. "They said I can stay the night if it's okay with you."

"Uh—" Mike looked at his niece, and Nicky's heart flipped as she saw some reluctance to leave in his eyes. "Okay."

He was about to stand when Stephanie and Lorry joined them. Lorry put the bottle of red wine she'd opened and replaced the cork on the table before them. Steph handed Mike a glass of wine.

"I'm sorry, I'm not going to be able to stay," Mike said apologetically.

"Nonsense," Lorry told him. "You stay there and enjoy some wine." She looked at Jade. "I can take you to Sam's house if it's okay with your uncle."

"I don't want to put you out," Mike said, taking the wine from Steph.

"You won't be," Lorry assured him. "I have to go anyway, and I was planning on seeing Sam tomorrow as I have something to talk to her about." Nicky's eyes narrowed. She could see her sister lying through her teeth. "Are you ready, Jade?"

"Is it okay to stop by my house to get some clothes?" Jade asked.

"Of course," Lorry said.

"Can you give me a lift home as well?" Steph asked Lorry. "And would you mind collecting the boys on the way?"

"Not at all. I have enough time before I fetch Gran from her bridge club." Lorry turned and smiled at Nicky. "Gran is staying at my place tonight."

"What?" Nicky looked at her sister, confused.

"Great, we'd better get going," Lorry said, waiting patiently for Jade to kiss and hug Mike goodbye. "I'll call you tomorrow." She pecked Nicky on the cheek.

"See you tomorrow, sis." Steph bounced her eyebrows mischievously at Nicky before kissing her on the cheek. "Have fun," she whispered.

Steph, Lorry, and Jade hurried to leave. Belvedere was right there with them.

"Belvedere, come here, boy," Nicky called him.

Belvedere stopped, looked at her, wagged his tail, gave a soft bark, and followed Steph out the door.

"Sorry, he looks like he wants to stay at my place tonight as well." Lorry grinned. "I'll bring him home with Gran bright and early in the morning."

Before Nicky could object, Lorry and Belvedere disappeared. An awkward silence descended over the deck when Nicky and Mike found themselves alone.

"Well, that was my sisters trying to not be obvious about leaving us alone in a romantic setting together." Nicky gave a small, embarrassed laugh. "I apologize for them and my dog."

"Don't worry, my niece played a part in that too," Mike told her, sipping the wine. "Mm, this is good."

"Yes, I brought it from Miami," Nicky told him. "It's one of the few things my ex-husband did right." She glanced at the bottle on the table. "He'd always bring a good bottle of red wine home from his trips around the country for my collection."

"You collect wine?" Mike looked at her quizzically.

"My father and I used to collect wine." Nicky gave a nostalgic smile, remembering her father. "It was our thing. We liked to send each other updates on our latest purchases and occasionally swap bottles. It was just—" She went quiet as how badly she missed him crept up on her. "Like I said, our thing."

"I understand," Mike told her, his voice filled with compassion. "Sully and I had a thing with rare books."

"Sully still has his rare book collection?" Nicky's eyes lit with interest. "I used to love going through it with him."

"I remember that." Mike smiled.

The ringing of Nicky's phone interrupted them. She leaned over and lifted it off the table. Her brow furrowed when she saw the caller was Megan.

"It's Megan," Nicky told him. "Excuse me." She answered the phone. "Hello, Megan."

"Nicky—" Alarm coursed through Nicky as she heard the desperation in Megan's voice. "Please, I need help. I've been having sharp cramping pains the whole day, and now I think my water just broke."

"What?" Nicky sat upright in the chair. Her wide eyes caught Mike's questioning ones. "We'll be right there. Just hang on, okay?"

"'What's wrong?" Mike asked as soon as Nicky hung up. "Megan's water broke, and I think she's in labor."

"Let's go," Mike said, bolting to his feet and pulling Nicky up with him.

CHAPTER 9

M ike paced the sterile hospital corridor, feeling like a fish out of water. He'd been at Physicians Regional Medical Center - Pine Ridge in Naples for a mere twenty minutes. Still, it felt like hours since they'd brought Megan in. Her water had broken and they were in the hospital awaiting the next steps in this whirlwind of events.

Nicky, calm and collected, was with Megan. She sat by her side, offering words of encouragement and comfort. Mike could see the determined look in Nicky's eyes. She'd had more experience with the arrival of new babies and was a pillar of support for the terrified Megan.

He, on the other hand, felt like he was stumbling through the unknown. This was his first time being responsible for bringing an expectant mother to the hospital, and he was acutely aware of his inexperience.

As he wandered the hallway, searching for a nurse or someone who could help, he thought about how Nicky seemed to effortlessly step into the caretaker role. It was as if she had a natural instinct for caring for people, whether it was animals, her family, or someone she'd not known very long. He admired her strength and composure.

Turning a corner, Mike finally spotted a nurse in pale blue scrubs at a nearby desk, shuffling through some paperwork.

"Excuse me," Mike said, trying to keep his voice steady. "I'm looking for some ice chips for an expecting mother. She's in room three-o-five."

The nurse, a middle-aged woman with kind eyes, looked up from her paperwork and gave Mike a warm smile. "Of course, dear. Just give me a moment to grab a cup, and I'll get you some ice chips."

Mike nodded, feeling grateful for the nurse's understanding. He watched as she swiftly prepared a cup of ice chips, her experienced hands moving with practiced efficiency. It was comforting to see someone who knew what they were doing.

As the nurse handed him the cup, she spoke softly, "Is this your first baby?"

"It's the daughter of an old friend." Mike nodded, suddenly feeling the weight of the situation. "But it's her first baby and mine." He shook his head as he realized what he'd implied. "The baby's not mine—" he corrected and ran a shaky hand through his hair.

"I understand." The nurse patted his arm reassuringly, her smile widening as she listened to Mike fumble through his sentences, trying to find words in his whirling mind. "Don't worry, dear. The doctors and nurses will take good care of her. It's a special moment bringing a new life into the world."

Mike managed a small smile, grateful for her words. He took the cup of ice chips and thanked the nurse before making his way back to the room.

When he returned to Megan's room, Nicky was still by her side, holding her hand and offering words of encouragement. Megan looked tired but determined, her eyes filled with a mix of anticipation and anxiety.

Mike approached Nicky, offering the cup of ice chips to Megan. "I got these for you."

Nicky smiled gratefully and took the cup. "Thanks, Mike. I'll take those."

Megan, her voice strained, managed a weak smile. "Yeah, thanks, Mike."

Mike pulled up a chair, sitting beside Nicky. He could feel the tension in the room, the palpable sense of waiting for something significant to happen. He wanted to be there for Nicky and Megan, even if he wasn't entirely sure how.

"Do you have children, Nicky?" Megan asked.

"No, unfortunately not." Nicky gave a tight smile, and sadness darkened her eyes.

"May I ask why not?" Megan panted as a wave of pain hit her, and she grabbed her stomach

Nicky talked her through the pain.

"I wanted children," Nicky told Megan, trying to calm the young woman. "But it wasn't meant to be." She smiled. "I can't have any, and before my divorce, I was going to adopt."

"Oh!" Megan winced. "I'm sorry, Nicky. I didn't mean to pry or make you sad."

"It's okay," Nicky assured Megan.

"I'm sorry to hear that too, Nicky," Mike told her, and Nicky nodded her appreciation. "I know it's not the same. But I can't have kids due to a hockey injury." He ran a hand through his hair as he blew out a breath. "It's one of the reasons I have two failed marriages." He gave Nicky an understanding smile. "My second wife and I were going to adopt, but—" He broke off the conversation. *There's no need to get into that part.* "It didn't work out."

"Oh, Mike, I'm sorry!" Nicky's eyes and voice were filled with compassion.

"It's okay," Mike said with a shrug. "I have Jade, and she's been an absolute joy."

"If you got married again, would you adopt?" Megan asked them.

"I would love to adopt even without being married," Nicky told her. "There are so many children in need of a good home."

"You're right," Megan grimaced again. "Ow!" She lay back against the pillow, panting. "I've decided what I'm going to do with my baby." She gritted her teeth and blew out a breath before looking at them again. "Mike, can you call Sam and tell her I need her legal counsel?"

"Sure," Mike told Megan, a frown creasing his brow. "Why do you need Sam's legal counsel?"

Alarm bells started ringing in his head as he put the pieces together, knowing that Sam specialized in family law.

"Because I'm nineteen." Megan rubbed her belly. "I want to be a doctor; as it is, I can barely keep the lights on at home." She sighed. "There's no way I can give this baby the life it deserves."

"What are you saying, Megan?" Nicky looked at her worriedly.

"I want to give her up for adoption." Megan's words startled Mike.

"That's a big decision to make," Mike said. "I'm sure you'll change your mind when you've held her for the first time."

"No, I won't," Megan assured him with a sad smile. "I've already decided on who I want for her parents."

"Oh!" Nicky and Mike said in unison.

"Nicky, if you're willing, would you take my baby?" Megan surprised them by saying.

"W... I..." Nicky stuttered, astounded by what Megan had just asked. She cleared her throat and gained composure. "Megan, are you sure about this?"

Megan nodded and swallowed as she started to pant in short breaths again. "Yes, I've never been more sure of anything in my life."

"Yes!" Nicky said with a nod, her eyes lighting with joy. "Of course."

"Thank you," Megan breathed before wincing again.

Nicky soothed and helped Megan through the contraction.

"I have one condition, though," Megan stated. "That Mike be her guardian if he's willing to."

Mike's eyes widened in surprise as he stared at Megan, dumbfounded by what she asked. His heart jolted and thudded against his rib cage. Most people thought being a guardian was just a title and taking on the responsibility, thinking nothing would ever come of it.

But Mike knew differently as he's lived through losing loved ones and having to take over parenting their most precious gift.

He swallowed, knowing he was gaping like an idiot. On the one hand, he felt honored to be considered, but on the other, he was terrified of what it meant. But the two women stared back at him, waiting for his answer.

"Of course," Mike blurted before he could change his mind.

"Thank you, both," Megan told them. Her eyes misted over. "You don't know how relieved I am." She grabbed Nicky's hand. "And I've asked your friend Mandy Oliver to handle the sale of Riley Cottage as I've decided to sell it to you, Nicky."

"What?" Nicky breathed, her eyes once again widening in surprise. "Megan, maybe you should wait until after your baby is born. I think Mike's right that you're making rash decisions at a moment like this."

"No, they're not rash," Megan assured them. "I've been thinking about this since I met you on the beach." She gave Nicky a warm smile. "I'll be giving my baby a wonderful mother with a big supportive family behind her." She leaned forward and closed her eyes against the pain before wheezing. "And my aunt would love that you're the one who bought the cottage."

"We can discuss this after the birth," Nicky told her. "Right now, you need to concentrate on your breathing and the little life you're about to bring into the world."

"No, talking is keeping my mind off the terrible fear gripping me about giving birth," Megan told her.

"You don't have to worry, honey." The doctor walked into the room. "We've got you."

Mike left the room with a promise to call Sam. Megan asked if Nicky would stay with her when the doctor told her it was time for her daughter to be born. Mike sat on a chair near Megan's room and called Sam, who answered on the third ring.

"Hello, Mike," Sam answered. "Is everything okay?"

Mike glanced at his wristwatch and saw it was pretty late.

"I'm at Physicians Regional Medical Center, where myself and Nicky brought Megan because she's about to have her baby," Mike told her.

"That's a few weeks early," Sam said. "Is she okay?"

"Yes, the doctors say everything is fine," Mike assured her. "Megan asked me to call you because you know she wants to give her baby up for adoption."

"Ah, yes!" Sam answered. "I haven't gotten the paperwork ready yet, and Megan still needs to ask —" She broke off.

"To ask Nicky if she'd take her child!" Mike finished for Sam.

"Has she asked Nicky?" Sam's voice was soft.

"Yes, and Nicky agreed to it, and I agreed to be the baby's guardian," Mike told her.

"Oh!" Sam went quiet for a few seconds. "Are you okay with that?"

"Yeah, why not?" Mike exhaled as he accepted the role.

"That's nice of you." Sam's voice was filled with admiration. "Tell Megan and Nicky I'll finish the paperwork and bring it through tomorrow."

"What happens to the baby in the meantime?" Mike asked.

"Well, as a close family friend, Nicky can take temporary custody of the baby until we can get the legal side sorted out," Sam explained.

"Doesn't Megan first need to see a counselor?" Mike was feeling concerned that Megan was making emotional decisions she'd regret.

"She has been seeing one," Sam surprised him by saying. "When Megan first approached me about wanting to give the baby up for adoption, I made her seek professional help. She needed to know what putting her baby up for adoption meant." She paused for a few seconds. "Megan really wants to be a doctor, and she wants what's best for her child, which she knows she won't be able to give her."

"That's basically what she said," Mike told her. "She also wants to sell Riley Cottage to Nicky."

"Yes, she told me that too." Sam sighed. "Megan wants to leave Marco Island and start a new life in Miami. It's where she's studying medicine. While Nicky is paying toward Megan's tuition, the sale of the cottage will help with the deficit and give her enough money to live."

"Megan sounds as if she's got it all figured out." Mike nodded, but his heart still felt heavy and blue for her. "I just can't help but feel so sad for her. I couldn't imagine having to give up a child."

"Megan is a courageous and intelligent young woman," Sam said. "I felt the same way you did, and I still do. As a mother, I go cold thinking about handing the life that has grown inside me for nine months to someone else and never seeing it again." She cleared her throat. "But I also know what it's like to try and study to reach your dreams with a newborn. I had Harry and both our parents to help us. Megan has no one. And becoming a doctor is a *lot* more grueling with terrible hours."

Mike hung up the phone after his conversation with Sam. He felt a mix of emotions swirling within him. The decision to become a guardian for Megan's baby had been a weighty one. Still, he couldn't deny the empathy he felt for her situation. It was a challenging choice, but it felt like the right one.

With his thoughts in turmoil, he began to pace the hospital corridor. Two hours passed like a slow-moving river. He couldn't sit still; the anticipation gnawed at him. Every step he took echoed in the empty hallway, a metronome of his restless mind.

The minutes ticked away, and the soft murmur of hospital activity became a constant backdrop. Nurses rushed by, doctors conferred in hushed tones, and the world continued to turn, even as Mike's life had taken an unexpected turn.

Finally, as if time had chosen this moment to relent, a nurse came to find him. She was a middle-aged woman, her face etched with the experiences of countless shifts. Her smile was warm, and her eyes held a reassuring twinkle.

"Mr. Sullivan?" she called gently, breaking through Mike's anxious thoughts.

He turned to face her, his heart racing. "Yes, that's me."

"The baby is here," she said with a soft smile. "Would you like to see her?"

Mike's heart leaped into his throat. He followed the nurse down a series of white-walled corridors, her footsteps echoing through the quietness until they reached the nursery. Through the glass, he saw Nicky standing beside a tiny crib dressed in protective clothing. She was peering down at the baby inside, a look of wonder on her face.

The nurse stopped and turned to him, a kind smile on her face.

"Mr. Sullivan," she said, "you'll need to wear protective clothing before we enter the nursery. It's essential to maintain a sterile environment for the babies."

Mike nodded, feeling a mixture of anticipation and nervousness. He followed the nurse into a small room adjacent to the nursery, where a table held a stack of pale blue gowns, gloves, and masks. It was a ritual he'd seen in movies but had never experienced firsthand.

As Mike struggled into the gown and pulled on the gloves, he couldn't help but feel the weight of this moment bearing down on him like an avalanche. It wasn't just about meeting Megan's baby; it was about stepping into a world of responsibility and commitment he never thought he'd encounter again. The memory of that pivotal moment when he'd agreed to be a guardian to Jade came crashing back with unrelenting force.

Mike had fallen in love with his niece the moment he'd met her when she was five weeks old. He could remember how his heart had felt like it had been blown up like a balloon filled with the purest love. Mike had been proud to think of himself as that little angel's guardian. Only then he'd pictured being a guardian as the cool uncle there when he was needed. And he had been that cool uncle until that awful day and the call that had shaken his world to its core. The shock of that moment still haunted him, slicing through his heart like a knife. He could recall the phone call as if it had happened just minutes ago.

"Mr. Sullivan, we're sorry to inform you, but your sister and her husband have been in an accident. They didn't make it, but their nine-year-old daughter did, and we need your consent as her legal guardian to operate on her."

The shudder that coursed down his spine was uncontrollable as the memories flooded back. He had been thrust into a nightmare that day, not only having to identify his sister and brother-in-law's lifeless bodies but also pacing the sterile halls of NCH Baker Hospital in Naples, waiting with bated breath for the outcome of Jade's operation. Just as he had paced the hospital halls earlier, each passing minute felt like a slow, agonizing descent into emotional torment on that dreadful day five years ago.

"Mr. Sullivan?" The nurse's voice broke through his turbulent thoughts. "Are you alright?"

"I'm fine," Mike replied, his voice trembling. "A little overwhelmed, I guess." He managed a nervous laugh. "This is my first experience with a newborn."

The nurse nodded in understanding. "Ah, yes," she said softly. "It's a feeling that defies description when you witness a brand new life, especially one that you're somehow responsible for or connected to."

As he followed the nurse into the nursery, Mike couldn't help but reflect on how life led you down unexpected paths. Each step he took toward that crib echoed with the enormity of the responsibility he had willingly taken on. It was a stark reminder that sometimes, life asked more of you than you ever thought you could give.

His heart pounded as his brain tormented him with memories. But as he stood beside Nicky, both of them dressed in protective attire, gazing at the fragile miracle before them, his heart melted. He swallowed the lump that had suddenly lodged in his throat, and all words seemed to leave him.

Mike and Nicky turned to look at each other. Her eyes mirrored the emotions tumbling around inside him. Nicky's eyes misted with tears as she smiled, a radiant expression that lit up the room and squeezed the breath out of him. Mike's already thumping heart lurched as he stared at her.

Nicky stepped closer and he could feel her body heat. Her soft scent tantalized his senses, her voice barely a whisper. "Mike, meet Riley." She gestured toward the crib, and his eyes followed the movement.

Riley was swaddled in a soft pink blanket. She lay peacefully in the crib. Her tiny fingers twitched, and she made a soft, contented sigh. Mike marveled at the fragile beauty of new life. Tears welled up in his eyes as he gazed at the precious infant. A rush of emotions washed over him—awe, love, and a profound sense of responsibility.

"She's beautiful." Mike's voice was raw with emotion as Nicky reached out and linked her hand to his.

"I can't believe she's here," Nicky said, her voice filled with wonder. "I can't believe Megan has entrusted her to us."

Mike nodded, his throat too tight for words. He looked at Nicky, and in that moment, he knew that his feelings for her ran deeper than he had ever imagined. It wasn't just about shared experiences, common interests, or a high school crush. It was something more profound, a connection that transcended the ordinary.

As they stood together, watching over Megan's newborn daughter, Mike realized that life had a way of surprising you. Sometimes, it threw unexpected challenges your way, and other times, it gifted you with moments of pure, unadulterated joy. This was one of those moments.

Mike knew he was embarking on a journey that would forever change his life. He and Nicky stood, their hands linked, sharing a few moments of silent understanding. In the soft, warm light of the nursery, fear and awe intertwined, creating a powerful, indescribable moment that would stay etched in his heart forever.

CHAPTER 10

Four Weeks Later

Nicky had spent the past four weeks navigating the unpredictable tides of her life. Baby Riley, whom she had unexpectedly become a parent to, had brought a wave of change she couldn't have foreseen. But she embraced it, and alongside Mike, they had been building a new rhythm to their days.

As she stood by the counter in the cozy bookstore, the scent of freshly brewed coffee and old books mingling in the air, Nicky couldn't help but let her mind drift back over these weeks. Mike had been a constant presence, not just in helping her with Riley but also in reshaping the store. The expansion of the bookstore's deck and the plans to transform the cottage into a coffee and trinket shop were taking shape with his dedication and hard work.

Nicky had to admit, much to her surprise, that she was grateful for his unwavering support. It wasn't just the physical work; it was the genuine care he had shown towards Riley and her. He'd taken to this role of guardian with a surprising ease, making Nicky wonder if he had any idea how endearing he was in the eyes of everyone they knew.

But beneath the surface of gratitude and the growing fondness for Mike lay a quiet storm of emotions Nicky had been avoiding. She'd been down this road before, and it hadn't ended well. There was something about him, his kindness, and the way he interacted with Riley that tugged at her heart. And she wasn't sure she was ready for that kind of vulnerability again.

As if summoned by her thoughts, Mike walked into the bookstore, a grin stretching across his face. His excitement was palpable, and Nicky couldn't help but respond with a smile of her own, pushing her internal conflict aside for now.

"Hey, Nicky," he greeted her, his eyes sparkling enthusiastically.

"Hey there," she replied, trying to match his enthusiasm, but her mind still raced with unspoken questions and doubts.

"You won't believe what I've managed to organize," Mike began, leaning against the counter.

Nicky raised an eyebrow, genuinely curious despite herself. "Do tell."

Mike's eyes gleamed. "For the grand re-opening of the bookstore, I've managed to secure a book launch of a number one best-selling mystery author."

Nicky's smile faltered momentarily, and she cleared her throat, her past colliding head-on with Mike's suggestion. "A book launch? That sounds... interesting. Who's the author?"

"Mitch Stone," Mike answered, oblivious to the sudden tension in the room.

Nicky felt like the air had been sucked out of her lungs. Mitch Stone. It was a name she had tried to erase from her memory. Her time working in the publishing industry in Miami had left her with a bitter taste in her mouth, and Mitch Stone was at the center of it all.

"Are you okay, Nicky?" Mike's concerned voice broke through her turbulent thoughts.

She blinked, trying to regain her composure. "I'm fine," she lied.

The name Mitch Stone brought a twinge of discomfort to Nicky. It was a name she'd rather forget, a name that had nearly cost her a promising career in publishing back in Miami. Despite the unexpected turmoil that surged within her, she managed to put on her best smile and asked, "Mitch Stone?"

Unaware of Nicky's history with the name, Mike responded enthusiastically, "Yeah, Mitch Stone. You know, the bestselling mystery author. I actually know his agent and Mitch himself quite well. His second mystery novel is about to hit the shelves. Having the launch right here at our bookstore could draw a ton of attention to Sully's Corner. It's just what we need to kick off the grand reopening with a bang."

Nicky's reluctance simmered beneath her smile. She'd never met Mitch Stone in person, and he certainly had no idea who she was. In her mind, she mulled over the idea. It was a practical move for the bookstore, but it meant dealing with a name she'd rather keep buried in her past. Nicky saw the excitement sparkling in Mike's eyes, and her heart lurched. How could she say no?

"I think that's a great idea," Nicky told him, hoping her reservations weren't mirrored in her eyes. "But it's a big undertaking when we only have a week until our grand re-opening of Sully's Corner."

"I know, and I'm sorry. I just want Sully's Corner to be as great as it used to be." Mike nodded and frowned, looking around the store. "Where's Riley?"

"My mother has her. She's taken her to her tennis club to brag about her new granddaughter." Nicky rolled her eyes. "That poor baby has been smothered with love and doting fans in my family, yours, and our friends."

"That's because she's so cute." Love shone from Mike's eyes as he spoke about Riley. "These past four weeks have been a bit of a learning curve for me." He gave a sheepish smile. "She's the first baby I've cared for."

"Oh!" Nicky's eyes widened. "I just assumed you'd have helped your sister with Jade as you seem so good with Riley."

"No." Mike's eyes widened, and he shook his head. "Jade was tiny, and I was so scared that I only held her if I was sitting down or one of her parents was close by."

Nicky laughed at the look of terror that flashed in his eyes while remembering Jade as a baby. "Then you've come a long way because you're fantastic with Riley, and she's also tiny."

"I know!" Mike agreed and smiled. "But I've had you supporting me, and Sam, your mom, and sisters barking orders like sergeants."

"I know, right?" Nicky shook her head in exasperation. "They've been like that with me too. They forget they were once first-time parents."

The room fell silent after Nicky referred to them as parents, and she saw Mike's eyes darken with emotion.

"Thank you, Nicky, for letting me have such an active role in Riley's life." Mike's voice was soft and hoarse.

"I don't know how I'd have coped without your support, Mike," Nicky told him honestly as her heart went wild as their eyes locked.

Belvedere barked from behind the counter, making them both jump as the dog shot toward the back doors, his tail wagging excitedly. They both turned to see Jade and Gemma on their way toward the store from the beach.

"I think you've lost your dog to those two." Mike laughed, breaking the sudden tension in the room.

"Them and Riley," Nicky added and said with pride, "I can't believe how protective he is over all the kids."

"He's a great dog," Mike told her. "And I'm not just saying that because he's the only animal that seems to like me."

"Ah, yes, your domestic animal curse." Nicky laughed, remembering Sam, Gemma, Harry, and Jade's stories about Mike and his bad luck with animals.

"Hi, Nicky, Uncle Mike," Jade and Gemma greeted as they entered the store before doting on Belvedere.

"We've come to take Belvedere out for a walk," Jade told them and looked around the store. "We're's Riley?"

"With my mom," Nicky answered.

"Aww," the teenagers' voices were filled with disappointment.

Jade put Belvedere's harness on, and before they left, she turned to look at her uncle. "Have you told Nicky yet?"

"No, I was about to," Mike said.

"Told Nicky what?" Nicky's eyes narrowed suspiciously.

Mike shared his and Jade's good news. "Jade and I are going to make Marco Island our home."

Nicky couldn't help but smile at the news. It was a significant change, but it meant more time with Mike and Jade, and she was more than happy to welcome them to the island.

"That's wonderful, Mike." Nicky looked at Jade, whose smile had widened. "I'm sure you and Jade will love it here."

"We do so much!" Jade's voice was filled with passion.

"We're looking forward to keeping riding with you too, if you don't mind, Nicky," Gemma said shyly.

"Of course, I don't mind," Nicky assured them. "I love riding with the two of you as well."

"And what about me?" Mike raised his hand, not wanting to be left out. "I thought I'd been doing quite well learning to ride Midnight."

"Yes, you have." Nicky laughed, thinking about the last four times she, Jade, and Gemma had gone riding, and Mike had joined them, insisting on riding Midnight.

"I think Midnight and I have become good friends," Mike stated proudly.

"You're lucky that Nicky asked one of the grooms to exercise him before we arrived at the ranch." Jade laughed.

"Or Nicky would've had to rescue you again," Gemma reminded him, and Mike pulled a pretend hurt face, grabbing his heart.

"That was one time." Mike shook his head and rolled his eyes. "And the first time I rode the beast."

"Maybe we can teach Riley to ride when she's old enough," Gemma suggested.

"I like that idea," Jade said.

Nicky's heart swelled. She also liked the idea of having them all in her life and glanced at Mike, her heart doing a few flips. Her attention was taken away from Mike when Gemma and Jade left.

Mike turned to her, his expression tinged with regret. "I'm sorry I have to do this," he began, a troubled look in his eyes. He pulled a face, clearly uncomfortable with the situation. "But I need to head to Miami for a few days to take care of some things."

"Okay!" Nicky felt a mix of emotions, but she managed to put on a reassuring smile. "Is it to do with your business in Miami?" she asked, her voice filled with genuine concern.

Mike sighed, his gaze briefly dropping to the counter. "That's one of the things I have to sort out in Miami," he admitted. "Before we came up here for the summer to deal with my uncle's estate, I was in the process of selling the business."

Nicky's eyes widened in surprise. "Oh!" she exclaimed.

"I need to get that deal finalized and also handle some matters with the house," Mike explained, running a hand through his hair in evident frustration. "I'm really sorry about leaving you hanging, especially since the book launch for the reopening was my idea."

Nicky waved off his apology, her support unwavering. "Don't worry," she assured him. "I've handled my share of book launches."

Mike appreciated her understanding, but he couldn't help but feel concerned about leaving her with so much on her plate. He glanced at his wristwatch and then back at Nicky.

"I'll be fine," she reiterated, dismissing his concerns. "Is Jade going to Miami with you?"

"No, she'll be staying with Sam," Mike replied. "Harry is coming with me, and we're driving to Miami together." He paused briefly. "Would you mind looking after them during the day when Harry and Sam are at work?"

Nicky nodded warmly. "Of course. Jade and Gemma can stay at Scott House whenever they want."

"Thanks," Mike said with a grateful smile. "I'll let them know. I'm sure they'd appreciate that."

Nicky's curiosity got the better of her, and she inquired further, "When are you leaving?"

Mike rechecked his watch and sighed, realizing that time was slipping away. "In... a few minutes," he admitted with a hint of regret. "Harry's meeting me at the cottage."

Nicky's response trembled with emotion. "Okay."

A soft smile crossed Mike's face, though it held a hint of sadness. "I'd better get to the cottage and get my stuff," he said.

Nicky nodded, understanding his reluctance. "I need to go home and fetch Riley," she offered. "I'll walk with you."

Mike's smile turned slightly gruff as he agreed, "I'm going to miss her and Jade."

With those words, he turned away to lock the front door. Nicky retrieved her purse and waited by the back door. Her heart raced as she watched him approach. He wasn't just handsome; he had a good heart, too. She swallowed hard, forcing herself to breathe as he drew nearer, their eyes never leaving each other.

He stopped in front of her, and unexpectedly, Mike whispered her name, and before she could react, she found herself enveloped in his arms. His lips crushed hers, and the world spun away, wrapping them in a dance of emotions as their hearts pounded out the beat. Then, all too soon, the song only they could hear ended as the sharp, shrill sound of Mike's ringtone broke the spell and dumped them back into reality.

Nicky felt a pang of sadness as she watched Mike reluctantly break their embrace. Her heart ached with the impending separation, and she tried to hide her feelings behind a forced smile. Her lips tingled with the imprint of his. Nicky felt giddy and breathless from their kiss. She stood dazed for a few minutes, staring into Mike's emotion-darkened eyes as his phone continued to ring insistently, pulling his attention away from their tender moment.

He sighed, his brow furrowing with a mix of frustration and responsibility. "Oh darn, it's Harry," he muttered, glancing at his buzzing phone. "He's at the cottage waiting for me."

Nicky nodded understandingly, even though her heart longed for him to stay. "You'd better take that and go," she said softly, trying to mask the disappointment in her voice.

Mike's conflicted expression mirrored her own as he answered the call. Their eyes locked for a fleeting moment before he nodded and turned away, stepping outside to speak to Harry, leaving Nicky standing there, battling the emotions that stirred within her.

Nicky quietly locked the store and slipped away onto the sandy path leading to Scott House. Her mind was a whirlwind of emotions, replaying that passionate kiss with Mike over and over again. Her heart sang with a newfound joy, and as she walked, it felt like it was beating to an entirely new rhythm. Each step felt light as if her feet weren't quite touching the ground, and she floated over the sand, carried by the intoxicating feeling of that moment.

"Nicky!" Lorry's voice dragged her from her thoughts as she looked up and realized she was almost home.

Nicky saw Lorry waving to her from the deck. She sat with Steph at the table with two large boxes in front of them and papers stacked in neat piles beside the boxes. As Nicky drew closer, she recognized the boxes as the ones Megan had left behind that were marked "Scott," and in which Nicky had found old receipts, photos, and a few financial log books.

"Is Mom back?" Nicky asked after greeting her sisters.

"Nope," Steph answered with a shake of her head. "Gran called and asked us to tell you they're taking Riley to the Granny and Me group."

"They've had Riley the entire morning," Nicky hissed, wondering if she was feeling separation anxiety because she missed Riley so much her heart felt bruised.

"We know that look!" Lorry told her.

"What look?" Nicky frowned at her older sister.

"The one where all you want to do is hold your child, breathe in their scent, and feel their warmth against you," Steph added with a knowing smile.

Nicky sighed. There was no use denying it. That's exactly how she felt; she couldn't have said it better herself. That, and this other feeling whirling inside her as the memory of the kiss she'd shared with Mike flashed through her mind. Her phone buzzed as if on cue, and Nicky pulled it out of her pocket. Her heart did somersaults when she saw a message from Mike.

We never got to say goodbye. I'll miss you and can't wait to get back to see you and the girls again... Oh, and Belvedere :-)

"Now that smile—" Lorry commented, "we haven't seen on your face in a long time."

Nicky's head shot up, and she felt her cheeks heat as her eyes moved from Lorry's knowing ones to Steph, who gave her a slow smile.

"What's all this?" Nicky cleared her throat, pocketed her phone, and changed the subject.

"The boxes you were going through from Megan's grandmother's cottage," Lorry told her. "I think you may have found where the mystery funds were going to."

"Oh!" Nicky's eyes widened as she pulled out a chair and sat.

"Yes, these log books are journals of money paid to the Rileys for the past seven years," Steph told her.

"Maybe it was a pension fund?" Nicky suggested.

"No, I've checked the amounts against the amounts paid from Dad's accounts," Lorry said. "The dates and amounts are an exact match."

"That must've been the funds paying for Megan's tuition," Nicky realized. "That makes sense. Megan said the funds stopped around the same time you changed the bank accounts, Lorry."

"We also found a lot of medical bills for Megan's mother that Dad paid for," Steph told her.

"Megan mentioned that her mother got sick, and we knew that already," Nicky reminded them. "Dad was helping Megan's mother with medical bills that her medical insurance didn't cover."

"It was more than that," Lorry told her and put some bills in front of Nicky. "Take a look at those. Her mother had to have extensive back surgeries and was on the organ transplant list for a kidney."

"It seems like Megan's mother didn't fall ill. She was in an accident," Lorry filled Nicky in. "We found the accident report."

"What has Megan's mother's accident report got to do with our family?" Nicky frowned.

"We don't know, but Dad covered *all* her medical costs," Lorry said, handing the accident report to Nicky.

"Then carried on paying until we put a stop to it," Steph continued.

"There's not much in this report." Nicky frowned, confused. "All it says is that Jackie Riley was involved in an accident."

"I know, right!" Steph's eyes widened in disbelief. "I've asked Sunny, a friend of mine who works at the police department, to see if she can find out anything for us."

"Why?" Nicky asked, putting the report on the table. Her eyes widened in realization. "Do you think that maybe Dad had something to do with the accident?"

"Why else would he cover all her medical costs?" Steph asked.

"Maybe because she worked for the hotel since she was twenty and was a good employee and a single mother," Nicky stated.

"This police report and the fact that Mom gets so angry when we bring up the mysterious payments," Lorry said, raising her brows, "tells me that there's a *lot* more to this."

Nicky frowned. Her eyes scanned the boxes. "What else is in these boxes?"

"Mainly just receipts. Medical tests. Medical records." Steph flipped through a few items in one of the boxes.

"There is a *lot* in them," Lorry told her. "It's going to take time to go through it." She looked around. "I say we don't let Mom or Gran know about this."

"Why?" Nicky asked again.

"Let's find out what we can first," Lorry said, shaking her head. "While we know that Dad didn't have a second family, he could still have had an affair with Jackie."

"Jackie?" Nicky gaped at her oldest sister in disbelief. "That's absurd. She was your age, Lorry."

"This happened seven years ago!" Steph's brow crinkled, and she thoughtfully bit the side of her mouth. "Something is nagging me about that time." She leaned forward and looked at the accident report. "The accident happened right before Halloween."

"Oh!" Nicky's eyes widened as she stared at Steph, remembering that Halloween. "That was the year—" She swallowed, and her eyes moved toward Lorry, who was looking at her curiously.

"The year that what?" Lorry asked, leaning her elbows on the table.

"Uh..." Nicky panicked and looked at Steph, who looked at her with wide worried eyes.

"Okay, you two." Lorry ran her index finger from Nicky to Steph. "Spit it out."

"We... Uh..." Steph looked at Nicky.

"That was just after you'd filed for divorce," Nicky hedged.

"Yes." Lorry nodded, her eyes narrowing suspiciously. "And..."

"The date on that report was the same day that your ex-husband, Grant, got into a bar fight and landed in the emergency room," Nicky's voice dropped.

She watched Lorry frown and take the accident report, then shake her head.

"His injuries never made sense for a bar fight," Steph pointed out.

"What are you saying?" Lorry asked them suspiciously. "You think Grant was somehow involved in this car accident?" She leaned back and threw the report on the table. "That's what Hannah said about his injuries. We all know our younger sister hated Grant, and besides, she's a psychiatrist."

"A psychiatrist who is also a trained trauma surgeon," Nicky defended their sister. "Hannah was convinced he'd been in a car accident, and his blood alcohol level was through the roof."

"Are you accusing Grant of causing the accident responsible for Megan's mother's injuries?" Lorry asked in disbelief. "Grant's a lot of things, but he'd never do something like this."

"Really?" Steph looked at her sister in amazement. "Didn't he kidnap his daughter to get you to change your mind about the divorce?"

"He didn't want to lose his family," Lorry defended him. "I'm sure any of us would react similarly if someone was trying to take your child..." Her brow crumpled into a tight frown, and her face fell. She closed her eyes and pinched the bridge of her nose. "No!" she whispered.

"Tell her," Steph hissed and kicked Nicky beneath the table.

"No!" Nicky whispered back. "No!"

"Tell me what?" Lorry's eyes were dark with emotion as she looked at Nicky.

"We saw Grant force a woman into his car that day," Steph blurted out. "We didn't see her, only that she had dark hair."

"What?" Lorry's face paled as she looked at her sisters in shock.

"The day of Gran't supposed bar fight," Nicky told her, "Steph and I were returning from the horse ranch when we saw Grant pushing a dark-haired woman into his car."

"The same car that he reported stolen the day after the bar fight," Steph continued the story. "You know the one that was never found again?"

Lorry nodded, looking ashen as their words sank in. "Still, why would Dad pay for everything?"

"Because Grant begged your father to help him," Pat Scott's voice made them turn to see her standing, staring at them from the back doors of the house. Riley was asleep in her arms. "It wasn't Grant's first DUI or the first time he'd hurt someone."

"I don't understand." Lorry's voice was barely a whisper, and Nicky's heart broke for her sister.

"Grant promised us he'd give you the divorce and not contest you getting full custody of Tammy," Pat admitted. "Your father had fired Jackie the day of the accident after finding out Jackie was pregnant with Grant's child. Grant and Jackie had been having an affair for three years."

"What?" Nicky, Lorry, and Steph spluttered.

"You and Dad kept this from me?" Lorry growled, her eyes filling with anger.

"Honey, if you're looking for an apology, I can't give you one," Pat told her, lifting her chin determinedly. "That man put you through hell, and your father and I could do nothing about it. He was your husband, and you loved him." She swallowed. "We were so relieved when you finally kicked him out of yours and Tammy's lives. But like a bad penny, he kept turning up, and at one point, we were so scared you would take him back." She cleared her throat. "What we did, we didn't do for Grant. We did it for you and Tammy. And as mothers, you all know you'd do anything to protect your kids, even if it means doing what we did."

"What happened?" Nicky asked, looking worriedly at Lorry who'd gone ashen.

"The day of the accident we found out about the affair Grant and Jackie had been having," Nelly, their grandmother, stepped out onto the deck beside Pat. "Your father was furious and fired Jackie on the spot."

"Jackie was distraught and begged your father not to fire her because she couldn't lose her job because of Megan, and she was expecting another baby," Pat told them. "That's how Grant found out about Jackie being pregnant. He overheard your father and Jackie arguing. He was furious and dragged Jackie out of the hotel before we could stop them."

"Grant was drunk. He'd been in the hotel bar," Nelly continued the story. "Before we could stop Grant, he drove off with Jackie. An hour later, we got a call from Jackie's mother about the car accident."

"Dad blamed himself for what happened," Lorry guessed. "He covered up the accident so Grant's parents wouldn't cut him off because he was already on probation with his family."

"Dad looked after Jackie," Nicky finished the story and glanced at the beautiful baby in her mother's arms. "And now we have Jackie's granddaughter."

"What happened to Jackie's baby?" Lorry asked.

"She lost it that day," Nelly answered.

"Your father, myself, and Nelly have been wracked with guilt since that day," Pat's voice was barely a whisper.

A stillness settled over them. All eyes rested on the tiny life sleeping peacefully in Pat's arms. Nicky realized the poignant twist of fate in the situation.

CHAPTER 11

It had been two days since Mike and Harry had left Marco Island, and he was itching to get back there. He missed Jade, Riley, and Nicky. A smile split his lips, thinking about their kiss, and his breath caught in his throat. She was like no one he'd met before. He'd known it since they were teenagers, and he'd first seen her curled up in an armchair in his uncle's bookstore.

"What's up with you, man?" Harry hit his hand on the table, jolting Mike from his thoughts and landing him back in the restaurant where they were having dinner. "You've been all—" He eyed Mike curiously. "Weird since we left Marco Island."

"I'm just excited to get back there and start a new chapter in mine and Jade's life," Mike lied.

"Uh-huh!" Harry nodded. "You seem to forget I've known you most of your life, and I can tell when something is up with you." He raised an eyebrow. "And something's definitely up with you."

"I'm just relieved that the sale of my business has been finalized." Mike leaned back in his chair. "And I'm worried about leaving Jade alone."

"Trust me, Sam has kept me updated, and the girls are having a great time," Harry said, grinning. "They went horseback riding yesterday and said it was so great not to hold back because of you," he teased Mike.

"Nice!" Mike gave his friend a black look. "I'm glad they're having a nice time. It's a relief."

"I have to take my hat off to you, man," Harry admitted. "You stepped into fatherhood not once but twice." He raised his beer in salute. "Sam and I are so proud of how you've helped Nicky with Riley."

"Thanks," Mike said, his heart doing that flip thing it did at the thought or mention of Nicky. "It's been life-changing my journey with Jade and now Riley."

"Yeah, life's funny that way," Harry said. "Just when you think you have it figured out, it changes course, and suddenly, you're floating down rapids totally out of control once again."

"I couldn't have put that better." Mike raised his glass and chinked it with Harry's.

"So, when are you going to reveal your big secret to Nicky?" Harry asked.

"The day of the book launch?" Mike pulled a face.

"As your best friend and knowing how you feel about her, even if you won't admit it, I have to advise you against that," Harry said. "Nicky's been through a *lot* with her ex, according to Sam. Which leads me to believe she might see your secret as a betrayal."

"A betrayal?" Mike looked at him, confused.

"You just springing your secret on her on the day of the grand opening and big book launch at your new joint business venture together is not a way to build a trusting partnership," Harry warned him. "That goes for a business, friendship, or relationship type of partnership."

"I'll tell her when I get back," Mike promised, taking what Harry said to heart, and he was right.

Over the past four weeks, as Mike and Nicky fixed up the bookstore and looked after Riley, they'd grown closer and gotten to know each other. Nicky had opened up to him about her ex-husband.

"There you are," a female voice that made the hairs at the back of his neck stand on end and his heart stop, came from behind him.

"Uh-oh!" Harry murmured. "Cruella de Ville alert." He looked at Mike. "By Cruella, I mean your ex-fiancée is heading our way."

"I got it!" Mike assured him.

"Hello darling," Gill Parson greeted Mike, bending down to kiss his cheek. "Your secretary told me you were here."

"Executive assistant," Harry corrected Gill and received a scathing look from her.

"Hello, Harry," Gill said flippantly.

"Hello, Gill." Harry's voice dripped with ice.

"Can you bring an extra chair?" Gill rudely stopped a server and demanded.

"We're nearly finished and are getting ready to leave," Mike told her.

"Oh, don't be like that." Gill pouted prettily. "I haven't seen you for months." She batted her eyelashes. "You haven't even called or messaged me."

"Gill, I told you I needed space," Mike hissed and caught the look of surprise in Harry's eyes.

"I think you've had more than enough space, darling," Gill purred. "When are you going to forgive me? I'm going to be leaving my father's company soon." She leaned provocatively closer to Mike. "I'm sure to be making a move to Star Publishers soon."

"That's not what I heard," Harry told her and got another scathing look.

"How would you know?" Gill hissed at him. "You're a plumber."

"Hardware chain store owner," Harry corrected her. "And my *brother* owns Star Publishers."

"A company that *I* put on the map saving your brother's failing publishing house and *your* friend's writing career," Gill gloatingly reminded Harry. "If I hadn't intervened and suggested Mitch Stone take his book to Star Publishers after that idiot of an editor working for my father turned his first novel down. Your brother's company would've gone bankrupt, and Mitch Stone would've faded into obscurity."

"Wow!" Harry whistled. "You really are as clueless as you look."

"Harry!" Mike admonished him.

"Please tell me you're not sticking up for Cruella again!" Harry's eyes widened. "You remember what she tried to do, right?"

"It wasn't her fault," Mike told Harry.

"Right!" Harry nodded, pushed his beer aside, took his jacket, and stood. "Dinner's on you," he told Mike. "I'll see you back at the house."

"Harry, wait," Mike said, feeling awful and guilty at not having told his friend the whole truth about Gill.

"Nope, don't worry about it!" Harry slipped his coat on. "The two of you obviously have a *lot* to talk about." He pushed his chair in. "Besides, I feel a need to round up all the stray puppies, especially the Dalmatians." He gave Gill a smug smile as she frowned at him in confusion. "I have a feeling they may be in mortal danger tonight."

With that, Mike watched Harry turn and casually strut out of the restaurant, leaving Mike alone with Gill. He knew he'd have a lot of explaining to do later when he got back to the house, and he knew that Harry would wait up for him, too.

"I know that man is your friend." Gill shuddered. "But honestly, darling, I have no idea why. The two of you are so different."

"Harry is a good guy." Mike's eyes narrowed. "Gill, what are you doing here?"

"I told you I was tired of waiting for you to call me, and I think you've had enough *space*," Gill said. "I'm tired of waiting around for you."

"Then move on, like I told you to," Mike told her. "Gill, I think you misunderstood me when I said I needed my space." He pulled his hands from hers. "We're over. I don't know how else to get that through to you."

"You said you needed space to sort your life out," Gill reminded him. "Not that we're through."

"Gill, please, it's been a long day, and I don't feel like arguing with you," Mike said resignedly. "I have to go. It's getting late, and I have an early start tomorrow as I have a lot to organize before returning to Marco Island."

"You're going back there?" Gill looked at him, surprised. "Why on earth would you want to go back?"

"I'm moving there for good," Mike blurted out. He hadn't wanted to tell her, but she brought the worst out in him, and he started to feel his stress levels rising. The woman was a viper. "Jade loves it there, and it was good to be back there."

"Is this because you still haven't forgiven me?" Gill asked him. "Because I told you a million times. It wasn't me that turned Mitch Stone's first novel down. It was that horrid editor that worked for my father." She tried to put her hand over Mike's again, but he pulled away. "She no longer works there, and my father was furious that we lost Mitch Stone's novels."

"Us breaking up wasn't just about the novel," Mike told her. "We don't work." He stood. "You'll have to excuse me because I must be going." He gave her a small smile. "Goodbye, Gill."

Mike paid the bill and left, not giving Gill a second glance as he walked into the humid Miami evening air. His mind swirled over all that had happened in the past five weeks as he walked back to his house, which wasn't too far from the restaurant in the upmarket neighborhood of Miami. As he neared his house, he saw the lights were still on and took a deep breath before going inside to face Harry.

Nicky's heart jolted every time the bookstore's door jingled or the glass door rattled. It had been five days since Mike had gone to Miami. He'd messaged her every day, and she was a nervous wreck, feeling like a giggly schoolgirl awaiting his return. Nicky glanced at the big clock in the shape of an open book that hung on the wall opposite the sales counter. Mike was due back in an hour. Her eyes fell on the boxes of Mitch Stone books that had arrived the previous day, which she'd promised not to open until he returned.

He'd told her there was something he wanted to tell her when he got back, and her mind had gone wild trying to imagine what that might be. She looked at the boxes of books again and then around the store. With the help of Sam, Gemma, and Jade, they'd managed to get the bookstore ready for the reopening and book launch. While Nicky was still nervous about meeting Mitch Stone, she was even more worried about Mike coming back. While they'd messaged while he'd been away, they hadn't seen each other since the kiss.

A knock on the door drew Nicky's attention, and she approached to see who it was. Her eyes widened in surprise at the sight of the smartly dressed woman standing there—a woman Nicky had hoped never to encounter again.

"What on earth is she doing here?" Nicky muttered to herself as she unlocked and opened the door.

"Nicky?" The woman attempted to look surprised, but Nicky knew better. This woman never did anything by chance. She had obviously heard that Mitch Stone was launching his new novel at the bookstore.

"Hello, Gill," Nicky said with a dry tone. "What brings you to my store?"

"Your store?" Gill pretended to be surprised. "I thought this store belonged to my fiancé."

"Sorry?" Nicky's heart sank. *Surely she doesn't mean Mike?* "For now, I co-own this store with—"

"Mike Sullivan," Gill finished for her. "My fiancé."

"Your fiancé?" Nicky looked at her in disbelief. "Mike is the man you gushed about nearly every day for the past year?"

"Yes, darling." Gill gave her a syrupy, sweet smile that Nicky recognized all too well. It was the smile Gill used when she was toying with someone. Nicky's heart raced, and she felt a wave of nausea wash over her as she realized she had allowed herself to get caught in another lying, cheating man's web. She gritted her teeth and forced herself not to show how torn apart she felt inside.

"Well, Mike isn't here right now," Nicky replied, trying to keep her voice steady. "He's still in Miami."

"Oh, that's okay," Gill said. "He wanted me to ensure everything was ready for his book launch."

"Yes, I have everything ready," Nicky said through clenched teeth, her hands curled into tight fists at her sides.

"Where are his books?" Gill glanced around the store.

"Mike asked me not to put them out until he got here," Nicky informed her. "He wants to set them out himself."

"Oh! That man." Gill rolled her eyes dramatically. "He's so particular about his book launches."

"Sorry?" Nicky frowned. "I wasn't aware that Mike had done a book launch before."

"How do you think he launched his last mystery novel?" Gill gave her a strange look. "I think it was more his good looks that sold two million copies of his book, though."

"Excuse me?" Nicky felt shock zinging through her as Gill's words began to sink in.

"It must be so weird for you," Gill continued. "You know, being the one who turned down his book and wrote that scathing review when it was published by another publisher."

Mike was Mitch Stone? Nicky's breath caught in her throat, and the world seemed to sway beneath her. She swallowed and forced herself to breathe, digging her nails into her palms to keep from passing out in shock.

"I'm not the one..." Nicky began to protest.

"That was you?" Mike's voice had her spinning around.

"Mike!" Nicky exclaimed as she met his stormy gaze, him standing there glaring at her.

"Oh, hello, darling," Gill exaggerated the term of endearment as she walked over to him and kissed him on the cheek. She then turned to look smugly at Nicky. "You didn't know Nicky was the editor who turned your book down and then nearly tanked it with her review?"

"What?" Nicky stared at Gill in disbelief, her emotions running wild.

Mike's eyes narrowed to slits. "Was that you?" he asked again, not taking his eyes off her. "You worked for Paper Tree Publishers?"

"Yes," Nicky nodded. "But I wasn't the—"

"Oh my goodness," Gill gasped. "Nicky, how could you keep something like that from Mike?" She feigned shock.

"Did you know I was Mitch Stone all along?" Mike ignored Gill.

"No!" Nicky rasped, her anger and hurt building up.

Anger surged through her, the pain of betrayals mixing with the heartache, and she felt it igniting within her. She glanced at Gill. "If we're keeping score of who kept the most secrets—" She shot a pointed look at Gill, her voice vibrating with rage. "You're way ahead of me there."

"Okay, I'm here!" Harry rushed through the door. "You can te—"

His voice trailed off as he looked at the angry faces of Mike and Nicky, then glanced at Gill. "Oh, you're here!" His eyes narrowed. "Stirring trouble again, I see."

"Oh, I'm not the one stirring here," Gill replied haughtily, smiling smugly at Nicky once again. "It seems Nicky here has been holding out on all of you. She's the editor who nearly ended Mike's writing career before it began."

"I know!" Harry surprised them all by saying, then walked over to Nicky. He put his arm around her shoulders and hugged her. "My brother will be forever grateful to her for saving his business—the one *you*, Gill, tried to sink."

"How dare you!" Gill gasped dramatically. "I was trying to help your brother. It's not my fault my father found out what I was doing and withdrew the funds I invested in Paul's business."

"Is that right?" Harry raised an eyebrow.

"Excuse me," Nicky said, stopping herself from breathing a sigh of relief when her phone bleeped with a message from her mother. "I have to go; Riley needs me."

Nicky turned and rushed to the sales counter to grab her purse and jacket.

"Is Riley okay?" Mike asked.

Nicky turned to leave and nearly collided with Mike, who was right behind her. She hadn't even heard him approach.

"I don't think that's any of your business," Nicky said through gritted teeth.

"I'm her guardian," Mike replied, his face resolute as he stood in her way.

"I'll see about changing that," Nicky seethed, then pushed past him.

"I'll ask Sam to help you," Harry told her.

"Thank you, Harry," Nicky said with a grateful smile. Harry's eyes were filled with compassion, and she could see that he, too, was angry with Mike and felt the same way about Gill as she did.

"Nicky!" Mike called after her as she rushed toward the glass doors, hoping her legs wouldn't give way as they felt like jelly.

"Let her go!" Harry told him, and Nicky saw him stand in front of Mike, preventing him from chasing after her.

Nicky turned and fled. She held her breath as she kicked off her shoes when she reached the sand. As her toes sank into its cool, welcoming depth, she pushed herself forward. Her mind reeled, and her heart felt like it was slowly shattering, like a beautiful ice sculpture hit by a chisel. She could feel the fine cracks running through her heart, and before she realized it, she was running toward her secret spot on the beach.

Her phone beeped once again, and she glanced at it, her hands shaking as she read her mother's message.

False alarm. Your grandmother had Riley dressed up too warmly. Riley is fine. We know you're busy with the bookstore, so we're taking her to the club. We love you, sweetheart.

Nicky breathed a sigh of relief upon learning that Riley was okay. She stood there, staring at her phone, her emotions churning inside her. Nicky longed to hold her daughter in her arms, but at the same time, Nicky felt as if she couldn't breathe from the pain tearing through her heart. She hadn't realized how deeply and quickly she'd fallen for Mike until Gill dropped her bombshell about Mike being her fiancé.

With shaky hands, Nicky dialed her mother's number.

"Hello, sweetheart," Pat answered on the second ring. "I'm sorry to have given you such a scare, but Riley is fine." She gave a nervous laugh. "Turns out your grandmother and I are a little rusty with newborn care, and we wrapped her up a little too warmly."

"That's such a relief," Nicky replied, fighting to keep her emotions under control.

"Are you okay for dinner tonight?" Pat asked.

"Yes, I'll be fine," Nicky assured her, although food was the last thing on her mind. "Are you sure you and Gran are going to be okay with Riley? You've been with her the entire day."

"Oh, we love having her with us," Pat told her. "Do you want us to bring her home?"

"No, it's okay," Nicky said. "I'll see her when you get home."

"Okay, sweetheart, we'd better get moving," Pat said. "I love you."

"Please give Riley a kiss from me, and I love you too, Mom," Nicky replied, her voice dropping.

She hung up and turned to look out over the ocean. The day was gradually transitioning into evening, bathed in a hue of golden pink. Nicky stood there, gazing at it, wishing she could turn back time to before she'd met Mike. Her world had just started to transition from dark clouds to bright, sunny days. Just as she let go of the tether she'd had on her feelings and let herself trust and believe again. A hurricane destroyed her newfound haven. As soon as she allowed herself to think about Mike, overwhelming emotions surged within her, and she collapsed onto the sand, tears flowing freely.

CHAPTER 12

"Y ou knew Nicky was the editor that tried to ruin my writing career?" Mike hissed. He felt numb inside. His mind was a fountain of confused thoughts.

"I knew Nicky worked for Paper Tree Publishers, yes," Harry confirmed.

"I told you!" Gill gloated.

Mike stood rooted to the spot. He couldn't believe that Harry had kept that from him.

"Why wouldn't you tell me that?" Mike ignored Gill. He was barely holding onto his anger as it was. He feared dealing with Gill would make him explode.

"It wasn't my place to tell you," Harry pointed out. "And, like Nicky said, you never asked."

"I'm asking now," Mike said through gritted teeth. "Was it Nicky who tried to get my book thrown out of nearly every publisher I sent it to?"

"No," Harry said, stopped, and corrected himself. "Well, yes."

"What is it, Harry!" Mike seethed. "Yes or no?"

"It's not as simple as yes or no." Harry's eyes narrowed as he turned them on Gill. "*Is it, Gill?*"

"I have no idea what you're talking about, Harry!" Gill told him and looked innocently at Mike. "I'm sorry this happened, darling."

"No, you're not!" Harry hissed. "You want the truth, Mike?" His eyes turned stormy as he looked at Mike.

"That would be good." Mike nodded.

"The first time you and Gill broke up, she put together this scheme to get you back," Harry told him.

Mike's brow knitted into a tight frown as his gaze dropped to Gill, who glared at Harry.

"Is there something you want to tell me, Gill?" Mike asked her.

"No, but your friend here is trying to drive a bigger wedge between us with more of his lies," Gill said in despair, her eyes filled with crocodile tears as she faced Mike. "Don't you see they just want you to hate me?"

"Oh, you pretty much did that to yourself," Harry informed her. "I spoke to your father after my brother nearly went bust because you withdrew the investment funds."

"My father did that," Gill stuck to her story.

"Should we call your father and his bank manager?" Harry pulled out his phone. "I'm sure we can conference them in." His eyes narrowed dangerously. "You were trying to make every publisher Mike had sent his books to turn him down. Only, you knew that my brother wouldn't bend to your threats. You knew he and your father were working on a deal to amalgamate the two companies and that Paul wanted to publish Mike's book. So, you tried to sink Paul's business." He shook his. "You couldn't have any publishing house take Mike's book. You wanted to swoop in at the last minute and publish it so Mike would be forever grateful to you."

"That's a lie!" Gill hissed. "Don't believe him, darling."

"Oh really?" Harry said. "Nicky may have written the review and turned your book down." He looked at Mike. "It was Gill that *forced* Nicky with the threat of Nicky losing her job and ending Nicky's career if she didn't."

"Is that true?" Mike's heart lurched, and anger boiled through him as he met Gill's wide eyes, and he could see, without her having to answer, everything Harry said was true.

"I did it for you!" Gill told him. "For us!"

"No, Gill, you did it for *you!*" Mike sneered. "I think you should leave."

"Mike, please, listen to me." Gill pleaded.

"Go!" Mike pointed at the door. His jaw clenched so tight a muscle ticked at the side. "And please don't ever come back because you're not welcome here."

Gill gasped. "You're making a big mistake!" She growled. "And good luck with little miss stuck-up Nicky." Her lip curled nastily. "But maybe you two deserve each other."

"Leave!" Harry's voice was laced with warning.

Gill huffed, turned, and pranced out of the shop, slamming the door so hard behind her that Mike was surprised the glass didn't break.

"You are such an idiot!" Harry hissed at Mike. "And Gill's wrong." He shook his head. "You don't deserve Nicky, and I won't be surprised if she never speaks to you again." He turned and made his way to the front door. "You'll be lucky if *I* ever talk to you again."

Harry stormed out of the shop but didn't slam the door as he left Mike standing, staring after him. His mind was a turmoil of confusion, regret, and despair while his heart ached. Harry was right. Mike was an idiot, and he most certainly did not deserve Nicky's forgiveness.

Mike closed his eyes and ran a hand over his face. What a mess he'd caused.

"Well, that was quite the scene," a female voice surprised him.

Mike's eyes shot open, and his head swiveled towards the sound of it. A tall, dark-haired woman was leaning casually against a bookshelf.

"How long have you been there?" Mike asked, his eyes narrowing. She looked familiar.

"Oh, since Harry came in," she answered.

"You're—" Mike was about to say, and she answered.

"Hannah Scott, Nicky's sister," Hannah introduced herself. "I came to surprise Nicky and meet my new niece." She folded her arms and tilted her head. "I know I should've run after her, and I was about to. Right after, I put you straight about a few things, but Harry did that for me."

"And you still didn't run after your sister?" Mike's frown deepened.

"I know Nicky," Hannah told him. "And by the look on her face when she left, Nicky didn't want to be around anyone, so I held back, and now I'm glad I did."

"So, you hid between the shelves and eavesdropped?" Mike's eyes narrowed accusingly.

"Pretty much." Hannah nodded, unabashed.

"Aren't you supposed to grow out of snooping on your siblings when you become an adult?" Mike raised an eyebrow.

"Snooping is not clothes or a phase a person goes through," Hannah told him. "It's something everyone does no matter their age."

"I'm sorry." Mike sighed and rubbed the back of his neck. "I don't mean to be rude."

"But you feel like you've just been dragged over hot coals?" Hannah guessed.

"Something like that." Mike let out a breath. "I'm sure you're dying to run and tell your sister what you've heard."

"Nope," Hannah said, shaking her head. "It's not for me to tell her." She pushed herself away from the bookshelf. "That's for you to do."

"Yeah, like Nicky's ever going to want to be in the same room as me, let alone talk to me ever again." Mike closed his eyes and clenched his jaw as the pain shot through his heart at the thought of Nicky and the look in her eyes as she fled from the bookstore. "Harry's right. I am an idiot." He grunted. "I let my ego get in the way of —" He ran a hand through his hand and looked at Hannah in despair. "What am I supposed to do now?"

"Well, when you're finished feeling sorry for yourself," Hannah said, walking toward him, "I'll help you."

Mike's brows shot up in surprise. "You'll help me?"

"That's what I said," Hannah replied.

"Why, after what I just did, would you want to help me?" Mike asked her.

"Because of how you're currently beating yourself up," Hannah told him. "And if I wasn't here, I have a feeling as soon as you caught your breath, you'd have been through those doors to find my sister."

"I'm that transparent?" Mike laughed.

"No," Hannah said. "You're just that guy." She smiled. "That guy who would weather a raging storm to try and set things right, especially when he knows he's in the wrong." She patted his arm. "It's stupid and sweet."

"I don't know what to say to that." Mike looked at her confused.

"Say, thank you, Hannah. I accept your help," Hannah told him. "And that you'll do what I say and not follow that big, soft heart of yours that I have a feeling will only lead you into more trouble."

"Thanks!" Mike's frown deepened.

"And..." Hannah rolled her hand to get him to continue.

"I accept your help," Mike repeated her words, and she rolled her hands again. "And I'll do what you say, not follow my big, soft, stupid heart."

"I didn't say your heart was stupid," Hannah corrected him. "I implied that it made you stupid and not think straight."

"I'm glad we straightened that out." Mike shook his head and rolled his eyes.

Speaking to Hannah made him feel better and a little hopeful that he could salvage his and Nicky's budding relationship.

"Great." Hannah's grin broadened, making him worry about what he'd gotten himself into. "I hope you're not doing anything tonight?"

"I had plans," Mike told her and gave another grunt. "But it looks like those aren't happening."

"If they were with Nicky, let's see if we can salvage them," Hannah said.

"I'm listening." Mike looked at her curiously.

"Good, because there's a lot for you to do," Hannah said. "And you might want to start by apologizing to your best friend, and maybe Harry and Sam will help you set it up."

"What about you?" Mike's curiosity grew.

"I'm going to organize Nicky," Hannah told him and looked at her wristwatch. "Let's aim for seven-thirty."

"That doesn't give us much time," Mike told her.

"Well then, you'd better get groveling!" Hannah gave him a smug smile.

· ♥ · ♥ · ♥ · ♥ · ♥ ·

"Nicky?" Hannah's soft voice broke into Nicky's quiet reflection.

Nicky had spent all the tears she had for the night and was now just sitting in the sand, letting the ocean's soft swish comfort her.

"Hannah?" Nicky quickly wiped the stray tears away and sniffed. "What are you doing here?"

"I came to visit my new niece," Hannah told her, dropping down next to Nicky. "How are things?"

"Oh, you know!" Nicky sniffed and forced a smile. "Fading into darkness." She laughed and indicated the day slipping away.

"Is that why you've been crying?" Hannah asked her with a worried frown. "You don't want the day to end?"

"I haven't been—" Nicky drew in a shaky breath and sniffed, knowing Hannah was the one person she couldn't fool. She sighed. "I did a dumb thing."

"You're not regretting adopting Riley, are you?" Hannah asked her.

"What?" Nicky looked at her sister dumbfounded. "No, of course not." She sniffed again. "Riley's the only bright thing in my life right now. Goodness, I could never regret that little girl coming into my life. She's my miracle."

"Then what's got you looking like your world is about to end?" Hannah's eyes widened. "The doctors haven't found any more tumors, have they?"

"No!" Nicky's frown deepened. "If you must know, I foolishly allowed myself to get close to a man." Her jaw clenched, and a burning pain ripped through her heart. "But, as usual, I chose a lying, cheating—"

"Okay, I get the picture!" Hannah held up her hands, then put her arm around Nicky's shoulders and squeezed her.

Nicky lay her head on Hannah's shoulder. She may have been the second youngest Scott sister, but Hannah was the wisest and always knew what to say to make a person feel better.

"Do you want to talk about it?" Hannah asked and planted a kiss on Nicky's head. "I've been told I'm an excellent listener."

"I should hope so." Nicky laughed, sitting up. "It's your job."

"Well, part of it." Hannah grinned and tilted her head, her expression becoming serious. "I'm here if you want to talk."

"I know," Nicky said with a grateful nod. "I'm just not ready to talk about it."

"Okay," Hannah accepted that. "But you know what I would like?"

"If it's to meet your new niece, you have a couple of hours to wait," Nicky warned her. "Riley is out with her grandmother and great-grandmother."

"Oh, no!" Hannah gave an exaggerated sigh. "Now, I'll never meet her."

"Don't laugh." Nicky sighed. "Mom and Gran are Riley hogs."

"Then why don't you take me and show me what you've done with that bookstore I found for you," Hannah suggested.

"I don't know," Nicky said, her heart jolting at the thought of returning to the bookstore.

"Come on." Hannah did the pleading routine, which meant she wasn't giving up on the idea, and Nicky would cave in before Hannah did.

"Fine." Nicky wasn't in the mood to try and win a round with Hannah. "But we'll have to be quick."

"Okay." Hannah shot to her feet and pulled Nicky up. She frowned and looked around. "Where is your faithful companion?"

"He, too, has found new companions," Nicky told her. "He's having a sleepover with Jade and Gemma."

"Gemma, as in Sam and Harry's daughter?" Hannah asked.

"Yes." Nicky nodded. "And Jade is Mike Sullivan's niece."

"Ah, okay," Hannah said, linking her arms through Nicky's and guiding her toward the house.

"Wait, I thought you wanted to go to the bookstore," Nicky said, pointing toward the way.

"Not with you looking like a melting Panda bear." Hannah pointed to Nicky's running mascara. "Good grief. I'll have nightmares taking you out looking like that."

"No one is going to see us," Nicky protested as her sister dragged her into the house.

"I will!" Hannah shuddered. "You know how spooked I get by running mascara." She gave Nicky a disgusted look. "It gives me the creeps."

Nicky sighed and let Hannah fix up her make-up, but stopped Hannah from putting gloss on her lips.

"No!" Nicky swatted Hannah's hand away. "That's enough." She shook her head. "I no longer look like a murdering panda bear. Now, can we go?"

"Sure," Hannah said.

They walked to the bookstore with Hannah regaling Nicky with stories about her life in Palm Beach.

"So, you're still going ahead with the wedding?" Nicky asked Hannah as they neared the bookstore, trying to keep her mind from flashing back to what happened there a few hours ago.

"Yes!" Hannah nodded. "This time, I'm certain Vincent is the one, and I can't wait to marry him so we can start our life together."

"Then I'm happy for you," Nicky smiled at her sister. "You deserve to be happy, sister. And if Vincent is the one that will make you happy, I'm happy."

"Thanks, sis." Hannah hugged her.

Nicky frowned when she looked through the store's glass doors and saw a soft glow.

"What is that?" Nicky was about to step forward to get a closer look through the glass door, but Hannah stopped.

"Okay, now don't be mad!" Hannah held up her hands. "But—"

Alarm bells started ringing in Nicky's ears. "What have you done?"

"Something you tend not to do," Hannah told her. "Give people a chance to explain."

Before Nicky could protest or flee, Hannah pushed the door open and dragged Nicky inside.

"Hello, Nicky," Mike's voice made her freeze.

Her eyes traveled to where he was standing behind a table set up with a candle and place setting for a romantic dinner. Her heart jolted, and her breath caught in her throat.

"No!" Nicky shook her head. "Nope!" She waved her hand through the air. "I'm leaving."

"No!" Hannah stopped her. "You're not."

"Yes." Nicky tried to dodge her sister. "I am."

"Nicky, please just hear me out," Mike asked her. "I know I don't deserve a chance to explain. I was an idiot earlier." He paused, and she looked at him. Their eyes met in the soft candlelight. "If you still want to leave when I'm done, I won't stop you." He ran a hand through his hair. "I'll give you the bookstore, and you won't see me again."

"What about Jade?" Nicky asked the first thing that popped into her head. "She's so excited about moving here."

"We'll stay here, but I'll move away from Tigertail Avenue," Mike said. "It is, after all, basically the Scott family's avenue."

"She'll stay." Hannah pushed Nicky toward the table, whispering to Nicky, "Stop being so stubborn. Mike is *nothing* like Grant the Gnat."

Nicky nodded and couldn't remember if she had walked to the table or if Hannah had pushed her. But she found herself seated in a romantic setting in front of Mike.

"I'm going to go!" Hannah said, bobbing like a meerkat looking for predators as she backed out the doors. "Play nice, you two." She pulled the doors closed behind her.

A silence fell over them as Mike poured them each a glass of wine and pushed one in front of Nicky. She took a big sip of the smooth liquid, trying to keep her eyes from locking with his.

"Nicky, I—" Mike broke off, sipped his wine, and gave a soft laugh. "For the past couple of hours, I've rehearsed what I would say." He closed his eyes and shook his head. "The truth is there's no words that can erase what I said or how I acted."

He swallowed and swirled the wine in his glass, watching it slosh from side to side before lifting his eyes to hers. Nicky swallowed. Her throat felt dry, and her heart felt frozen as she held her breath. She could see the flickering flame of the candle dance in his eyes as she stared, being drawn into their warm depths.

"I know it's worth nothing; actions speak louder than words." His voice was barely audible and was gruff with emotion. "I'm so sorry I acted like a jerk." He squeezed his eyes shut, and Nicky could feel his pain resonate through her.

While her heart screamed for her to forgive him, her mind wasn't so quick to let him off the hook. Mike had kept secrets from her and had judged her without giving her a chance to explain.

"I want to say it's okay," Nicky's voice shook with suppressed emotions. "But it's not." She shook her head, and her eyes dropped to the glass of wine before they drifted shut as she composed herself. "You hurt me." She looked at him. "I thought you were different." She gave him a small smile. "Then Gill breezed in here and told me you and she were engaged."

"Were being the operative word," Mike assured her. "Gill and I were over a long time ago. She just took a while to accept it."

"I couldn't believe you were *that*, Mike," Nicky told him. "It was an even bigger shock to discover you were Mitch Stone." She swallowed the emotion, trying to spill over, but it refused to stay down, and she felt her eyes sting with tears. "I'm sorry, Mike." She sucked in a shaky breath trying hard not to cry. "I thought your book was brilliant—"

"I know!" Mike reached across the table, took her hand, and Nicky let him. "Harry told me everything."

"How did Harry know?" Nicky looked at Mike, confused for a few seconds before it dawned on her. "That's right, his brother owns Star Publishers." She wiped a stray tear from her cheek. "I would never try and do such an awful thing to any writer. Good or bad."

"I know!" Mike nodded. "Deep down, this afternoon, I knew then too." He blew out a breath. "Where you're concerned, my emotions are heightened," he admitted, and their eyes collided in a heart-stopping moment. "Nicky, I've never felt this way about anyone. I'm so hopelessly in love with you. It's what I've needed to say for so long that I couldn't think straight."

His words sent an electric shock through her system and straight to her heart. Making it try to bounce out of her chest to join his. She took a breath and smiled at him.

"I'm in love with you too." Her voice was barely a whisper but filled with love. "I've never felt the way I did when I thought you were with Gill."

"I'm sorry, Nicky." Mike took both her hands. "Please tell me what I can do to make it up to you."

"How about we agree to no more secrets?" Nicky gave him a shaky smile.

"I can agree to that." Mike nodded.

Before Nicky could say another word, Mike was out of his chair and pulling her into his strong arms. His lips met hers, and her world clicked back into place before fading away to leave only them as they got lost in each other's embrace.

Nicky didn't know how long before they came up for air and stood wrapped in each other's arms.

"Nicky, what would you think about us becoming a family?" Mike whispered in her ear. "I don't just want to be Riley's guardian. I want to be her father and your husband."

Nicky's eyes widened as she drew back to stare into his eyes, burning with emotion.

"Will you marry me?"

Nicky's heart raced wildly in her chest as she stared at him. As his lips turned into a warm smile, Nicky knew that this was where fate had been guiding her to—home. And home was with this man who now had her heart.

"Yes!" Nicky said before Mike claimed her lips once again.

CONTINUE THE SERIES

SCOTT SISTERS SERIES - BOOK 2

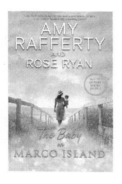

THE BABY ON MARCO ISLAND

CHAPTER 1

The warm Florida sun hung high in the sky, casting a shimmering brilliance over Marco Island. It was the kind of day that postcards were made of, where the sea and sky melded seamlessly, and the world seemed bathed in golden light. Seated at a quaint seaside restaurant, Stephanie Victor, affectionately known as Steph, savored the view as much as her grilled shrimp salad. She felt a sense of contentment at the moment—a rare luxury in the whirlwind of her daily life.

Across the table, her younger sister, Hannah, stirred a lemon wedge into her water, her fingers dancing in the brilliant glare. With Hannah's long, dark, auburn hair and cool poise, she had the unmistakable air of a woman in control. Despite the informal lunch setting, her aura was one of elegance, the kind of presence that made everyone take notice.

Steph regarded her sister over the rim of her iced tea glass, her pale blue eyes filled with curiosity and concern. "So, this is the third surprise visit you've paid us in the space of three months." She took a sip of water. "What's going on, Han?"

Hannah offered a serene smile, her deep violet eyes holding their own secrets. "I needed a break from the Palm Beach hustle, Steph. Vincent has been swamped with surgeries, and well, you know how stressful that and my work can be."

Steph leaned back in her chair, studying her sister intently. "Is that all it is? Just a breather?"

Hannah's gaze flickered, a barely discernible hesitation in her response. "It's mainly that, but..." She let her words trail off.

Steph's brows furrowed. She knew her sister well, and these half-finished sentences clearly indicated that something else was bothering Hannah. "Hannah, you can talk to me. I'm your sister, you know."

Hannah sighed, her violet eyes holding a mixture of frustration and relief. "Alright, alright. It's not just about taking a break. Vincent and I, well, we've been having some issues lately."

Steph's heart went out to her sister. Hannah had a history of faltering on the doorstep of marriage, having gained a somewhat notorious reputation as the "runaway bride" in the Scott family. Despite her successful career as a psychiatrist, her love life had been nothing short of tumultuous. "What's going on? Are you having second thoughts again?"

Hannah shook her head, and her gaze showed genuine weariness. "It's not that. I do love Vincent. He's a wonderful man. But lately, I've been feeling somewhat suffocated with his schedule and all the stress. It's as if I'm being swallowed by this relationship."

Steph understood the dilemma. The prospect of losing her independence was daunting. "Have you talked to him about this?"

"We've had some heated discussions," Hannah admitted. "He's worried that I'm going to call off the wedding, and it's putting even more pressure on us."

Steph reached across the table, placing her hand over Hannah's. "Marriage is a partnership, sis. It's about finding that balance between love and freedom. You know that."

Hannah offered a weak smile, her eyes finally revealing the vulnerability she had been keeping hidden. "I know you're right, Steph. I just needed a breather to think things through."

Steph patted her sister's hand, offering her silent support. "Well, you're here now, and we're going to enjoy our time together. No heavy discussions today."

Hannah nodded in agreement, her features relaxing. "You're right. I came here to escape the drama, after all."

They returned to their meal, the sun-drenched coastline a soothing backdrop to their sisterly reunion. The restaurant bustled with chatter and the aroma of fresh seafood. As they savored their lunch, Steph couldn't help but feel a sense of contentment at having her sister by her side.

After lunch, they strolled back to Hannah's car. The air was warm and thick with the scent of saltwater. The brilliant cerulean of the Gulf of Mexico stretched out before them, a serene backdrop to their sisterly conversation.

As they approached the car, Steph felt an unexpected rush of dizziness, her surroundings blurring around her. Her steps faltered and her knees weakened. Her vision tunneled, and she collapsed into the passenger seat of Hannah's car just in the nick of time, her consciousness fading.

The world went black.

Steph awoke to the sterile scent of a clinic. The overhead lights were harsh, and her head throbbed with a dull ache. As her eyes adjusted to the brightness, she realized she was lying on a crisp white examination table.

Hannah sat beside her, her dark red hair a soft cascade around her worried face. "Thank goodness you're awake." She breathed a sigh of relief.

Steph's voice was hoarse. "What happened?"

Hannah offered a gentle, reassuring smile. "You fainted, Steph."

The room felt too white, too sterile. Steph blinked, struggling to understand. "Fainted? Why?"

Hannah reached for her hand. Her violet eyes filled with concern. "I'm not sure. But we're going to figure it out. The doctor is running some tests." She glanced around the room. "This small clinic is remarkably well equipped."

Steph blinked, the stark whiteness of the room sending a chill down her spine. Her head was heavy, and her thoughts scattered like leaves in the wind. Hannah's words swirled in her mind, and she fought to comprehend them.

The room's clinical sterility contrasted with the warmth and brightness of the day outside. She tried to sit up, but dizziness washed over her like a crashing wave. The hospital bed felt alien, unfamiliar. The fluorescent lights stung her eyes, and the sterile aroma intensified her discomfort. Hannah's violet eyes held worry and care.

"What kind of tests?" Steph asked as she tried to make sense of her surroundings. She had no recollection of how she ended up here, her mind clouded by the disorienting moment of her collapse.

"The doctor drew some blood and asked me a whole lot of questions." Hannah grinned and patted Steph's arm. "Don't worry. He's sure it's just the heat and maybe the shellfish you had for lunch."

"I have food poisoning?" Steph frowned and allowed Hannah to help her into a sitting position.

"Could be." Hannah nodded and pulled a face. "I'm sorry. I know you wanted to go to that other restaurant, but I really wanted to try that new seafood place."

"It's not your fault, Han." Steph drew in a few deep breaths, trying to steady herself. "Is there some water?" Her stomach started to roil as bile crept up her throat. "Oh, no, I think I'm going to be sick."

"Here!" Hannah jumped up and grabbed a bedpan, holding it out for Steph.

But after a few seconds of leaning over the bedpan, the feeling faded.

"I think it must've been the shellfish salad." Steph nodded, holding her protesting stomach. "Especially after I've been on a strict diet to set my system right."

"Steph!" Hannah moaned at her, shaking her head. "What is up with you lately?" Her brow furrowed worriedly. "You've never been into fad diets or trying to get into shape." She ran an eye over her sister. "I don't think you can get into better shape than you already are." She gestured with her hand. "You always do yoga, run, and swim. You're gorgeous and don't need these fad diets."

"It's not a diet," Steph protested. "It's a lifestyle change. I'm forty-three. I have to start changing the way I do things."

"Okay," Hannah held up her hands in surrender. "Just don't push yourself into a skeleton."

"It's not that kind of diet," Steph assured her and looked around the room. "I hate doctors' offices."

"I know," Hannah told her. "But you collapsed, and I wasn't taking any chances."

"Thank you, Han." Steph smiled warmly before glancing impatiently at the door. "Where is the doctor? I have to collect the twins soon."

"Lorry is going to collect them," Hannah told her.

"Oh, no." Steph looked pained. "You told the family I'm at the doctor?"

"No, I told our oldest sister you were at the doctor," Hannah said. "After Lorry called me to find out where you were and when you were getting back to the hotel."

"Of course." Steph shook her head. "Because It's my turn to collect the kids from the horse ranch."

"Not anymore, it's not." Hannah pursed her lips and raised her eyebrows. "I told Lorry you may have food poisoning, so she's gone to fetch them and said you must take the rest of the day off."

"Awesome!" Steph sighed, knowing she would be bombarded with calls from the other four of her sisters, her mother, and her grandmother to find out how she was. "My afternoon isn't going to be easy now, fending off calls from the family finding out how I am."

"Aren't you staying at Scott House pool house while your house is being renovated?" Hannah asked.

"Yes," Steph confirmed.

"Well, then, as soon as you get back to Scott House, you can tell everyone all at once how you are," Hannah pointed out. "And I'll call Ashley and Jess to let them know after the doctor has told us what is up with you."

"Thanks, sis," Steph said as she sighed in relief, suddenly feeling terribly tired.

Hannah's phone rang and she pulled it from her pocket.

"Oh, It's Vince." Hannah pointed at the phone. "I have to go outside the clinic to take this." She looked at Steph questioningly. "Are you going to be okay?"

"Of course." Steph waved her off.

As Hannah left the room to take a phone call, the air in the small examination chamber felt close and confined. The hum of fluorescent lights and the occasional clatter of a distant gurney filled the silence.

Steph sat back with her feet stretched in front of her. Her thoughts drifted through the haze. With Hannah out of the room, she had a moment to absorb her peculiar situation. What could have caused her to faint? Her health had been relatively stable, and she didn't remember feeling ill before the incident.

The door swung open and a doctor entered. He wore a white coat that rustled softly with his movements. His features were kindly, and his eyes held a warmth that put Steph at ease.

"Good afternoon, Ms. Victor," the doctor greeted her, checking her chart. "I'm Dr. Reynolds. Your sister mentioned that you fainted?"

Steph nodded, her voice a mere whisper. "I did, but I don't know why."

Dr. Reynolds proceeded to ask her a series of questions about her health, any recent changes in her life, and her medical history. Steph provided what answers she could, but her memory was muddled.

After some discussion, the nurse called Dr. Reynolds away to get Steph's test results. As he left the room, Steph couldn't shake the lingering unease. Why had her body betrayed her like this?

The minutes dragged on, and Steph felt a growing sense of isolation. The silence in the room pressed in on her, and she closed her eyes, trying to find solace in the darkness behind her lids.

When Dr. Reynolds returned, he carried a folder in his hand. The expression on his face was more serious than before, a hint of concern in his eyes.

"Ms. Victor, I have the results of your tests," he began gently. "Your vitals seem stable, and we couldn't find any immediate health concerns."

Steph's brow furrowed. "So, why did I faint?"

Dr. Reynolds paused for a moment as if choosing his words carefully. "During the tests, we discovered something else."

Steph's heart skipped a beat. "What do you mean?"

The doctor's expression softened into a kind smile. "Ms. Victor, you're eight weeks pregnant."

The word hung in the air, and the room suddenly charged with a mixture of shock and disbelief. Steph's mind raced. She was pregnant? The news felt like a thunderbolt, an unexpected revelation that turned her world upside down.

Eight weeks pregnant. Steph couldn't believe it. The realization struck her like a sudden storm. Then, a memory flickered through the haze of her thoughts. The Bahamas trip that Max had surprised her with nine weeks ago. The romance of that vacation, the shimmering waters, and starlit nights, the tender moments between her and Max. Could this be the result of that trip?

Steph's hands trembled as she placed them on her abdomen as if trying to comprehend the life growing within her. A mixture of emotions swirled within her—surprise, fear, and a hint of something else she couldn't quite define.

As Steph waited in the reception area for Hannah to return from her long telephone conversation, anxiety gnawed at her. Her mind raced and her emotions were in turmoil. She wasn't ready to tell her family about this yet. She had her own relationship woes, and Steph wasn't sure if this was the right moment to share her own unexpected news.

When Hannah returned, her red hair flowing like a river of fire, she looked at Steph with expectant eyes. "What did the doctor say?"

Steph's voice wavered. "I need some supplements for the dizziness, but it's nothing serious. I'm just a little dehydrated, and you were right—it's probably that crazy diet. I also have an appointment for a checkup soon. I have to take it easy for the rest of the day."

Hannah nodded, concern evident in her violet eyes. "Good to hear. We should get you back home, then."

Steph hesitated for a moment, her mind a battlefield of emotions. Then, she managed a faint smile and averted her gaze. "Hannah, when we get to Scott House, would you please let everyone know? I want to go straight to bed. I think I need a little time to myself today."

Hannah regarded her sister with understanding. "Of course, Steph. You know where to find me if you need anything."

As they left the clinic, Steph's mind raced with thoughts of the tiny life growing inside her. Her world had shifted dramatically in a matter of hours, and she needed time to process this newfound reality on her own. Her family's reactions could wait. For now, she wanted to come to terms with this life-changing news privately.

Steph leaned back in the passenger seat of Hannah's car as the familiar sights of Marco Island passed by. The sunny streets, lined with palm trees, felt different now. The world had shifted, taking on a new dimension she couldn't quite grasp.

As they pulled up to Scott House, Steph felt a mixture of relief and trepidation. Her family's support was unwavering, and she knew she could rely on them if needed during this unexpected journey. Only Steph wasn't too sure what that journey would be right now.

She turned to Hannah and managed a weak smile. "Thank you for everything today, Han. I'll see you soon."

Hannah reached out and squeezed her sister's hand. "Take your time, Steph. I'll let everyone know."

With a heavy heart, Steph stepped out of the car, took a deep breath, and began the short walk to the pool house. The lush garden surrounding her was in full bloom, a riot of colors and fragrances. For a moment, the beauty of her family's home provided a soothing backdrop to the tumult of emotions inside her.

Entering the pool house, the memories of the past flooded her mind. The spacious living room was adorned with photos, capturing moments of laughter, love, and family gatherings. Steph's gaze settled on one particular picture, a snapshot of her twin sons, Jack and Liam, from a few years ago. They were inseparable, their faces radiating pure mischief and joy. She sighed, thinking about how they'd react to the news of a new sibling.

But as her fingers brushed the photograph's surface, her mind wandered back to a time of profound struggle that had cast a long shadow over her life.

Fourteen years ago, her life had nearly been shattered during her first pregnancy. What should have been a time of excitement and anticipation turned into a harrowing ordeal. She remembered the terror, the uncertainty, and the relentless pain.

Steph was in her twenties, blissfully in love with Max, and full of dreams. The anticipation of becoming parents had filled their days with joy. But then came the complications. The medical terms had blurred into a dizzying maze of confusion, and the doctors' faces had lost their reassuring smiles.

Her high-risk pregnancy had escalated into a nightmare. Max, a firefighter and paramedic at the time, was her pillar of support through the turbulent months. But even his unwavering strength had faltered in the face of a situation neither of them was prepared for.

She remembered the day they rushed to the hospital. The emergency room was a blur of frantic doctors and nurses. The twins were coming prematurely, and the risks loomed large.

Steph had been on the verge of losing both her children, the very thought, a devastating weight on her heart. The memory of their fragile, newborn forms filled with tubes and wires was etched deep within her soul.

The twins' survival was a miracle, but the experience had taken a toll on Steph. It wasn't just the twins' lives that had been under threat as Steph suffered from postpartum hemorrhage that nearly took her life. It was not just her body that had been scarred; it was her spirit. While she'd heard all the beautiful stories of pregnancy and childbirth from family and friends, all Steph could remember was the terror and pain. And now, faced with the prospect of another high-risk pregnancy, those old fears resurfaced like relentless ghosts from the past.

Steph made her way to the bedroom, her heart heavy with the burden of these memories. She lay on the bed, the room bathed in soft, golden light from the large window overlooking the garden. Her thoughts drifted back to the present, to the tiny life growing inside her, and she wrestled with the uncertainty of her marriage.

Max, once her rock, had been slowly drifting away since the incident that forced his early retirement as a firefighter. Their relationship had become fragile, teetering on the precipice of something unknown. Steph had long felt the strain. Still, she'd been reluctant to address it, fearing it might shatter the illusion of their picture-perfect family life.

Now, with the weight of her unexpected pregnancy adding to the turmoil, she was faced with choices she wasn't sure she'd ever be prepared to make. The uncertainty was unbearable, and she drifted into a restless sleep, hoping that her dreams might offer some clarity or respite from the decisions looming on the horizon. The journey ahead would be fraught with challenges and uncertainty.

AVAILABLE TO ORDER NOW ON **AMAZON**

SCOTT SISTERS SERIES

Series Books:

The Beach Hotel on Marco Island – Prequel

The Bookstore on Marco Island – Book 1

The Baby on Marco Island – Book 2

The Bachelor on Marco Island – Book 3

The Restuarant on Marco Island – Book 4

The Studio on Marco Island – Book 5

The Bride on Marco Island – Book 6

AVAILABLE ON **AMAZON**

ALSO FROM AMY RAFFERTY

SWEET COLORADO ROMANCE

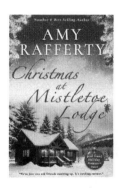

CHRISTMAS AT MISTLETOE LODGE — BOOK 1

"Walking away from you, leaving you standing there at the altar... it tore me apart. But I thought it was the right thing to do."

Avery Hawthorne left behind a lot when she moved to California.

Her family, the familiarity—and a small-town romance with an enigmatic ex she's tried to forget.

As the holidays roll around, she's determined to earn a promotion from her boss and make the sacrifices all worth it.

But this new task means going back to the place she fled twelve years ago.

Her boss is confident the deal for Mistletoe Lodge will be easy. The owners are drowning in debt and Avery has 'history' with the Carlisle family. What he doesn't know is that her history with them is anything but good.

Avery's ex, Ryder Carlisle, is determined to keep his family's inn afloat and has ideas to revamp it. The last thing he wants is to give in to some big corporate hotel chain. But he never imagined they'd send the one person he couldn't say "no" to!

Avery just wants to celebrate Christmas with a promotion.

Ryder wants to keep Mistletoe Lodge in the family.

In a battle of wills over Christmas festivities, Avery and Ryder reignite old flames as they wrestle with their wills—and their own feelings, which remain just as strong twelve years later.

It was official. Fate really had hijacked her festive season and was busy toying with her...

CHRISTMAS AT MISTLETOE LODGE is Book 1 of the Feel Good Holiday Romance series, a powerful women's fiction saga in which Avery and Ryder have a second chance at romance if they can push aside their stubbornness and the wrongs of the past...

AVAILABLE ON **AMAZON**

COMING SOON FROM AMY RAFFERTY

COBBLE BEACH ROMANCE SERIES - BOOK 1

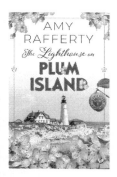

THE LIGHTHOUSE ON PLUM ISLAND

CHAPTER 1

Caroline Shaw's heart raced with exhilaration after her meeting with Travis Danes. As she strolled through the bustling streets of New York alongside her lifelong friend, Jennifer Gains, palpable excitement filled the air. Travis had wholeheartedly agreed to her terms, and within three to six months, a film crew would descend on Plum Island to bring her beloved "Cobble Cove Mysteries" to life on screen. It was a dream unfolding before her eyes.

"Can you believe it, Jen?" Caroline gushed, her hazel eyes sparkling with joy. "He actually agreed to everything! The film crew will be on Plum Island soon, and we'll be making magic together!"

Jennifer, who had been Caroline's unwavering source of support since childhood, beamed in response. "I always knew you could do it, Caroline. Your writing is brilliant, and now the world will not only read your work but see it come to life."

Their destination was Jennifer's favorite coffee shop in Soho, a haven of creativity and conversation. Just as they arrived at the charming spot, Jennifer's phone rang, and she sighed regretfully.

"It's work," Jennifer said apologetically. "I'm so sorry, Caroline. I have to take this."

"No worries," Caroline replied with a reassuring smile. They were close to the cafe entrance, and she gestured for Jennifer to go ahead. "I'll have a coffee and write while you handle business. We can catch up later at your place for our celebration dinner."

Jennifer made sure the owner of the coffee shop noticed them and guided Caroline to her usual table by the window before rushing off to attend to her call. Caroline settled into her seat, and Simon Newbury, the cafe's owner, greeted them warmly.

"Good afternoon, ladies," Simon said with a charming smile. "You both look lovely today."

"Thank you, Simon," they chimed in unison, and Caroline took a menu.

"Why are you still standing?" Simon inquired with a quizzical look at Jennifer.

"Because I have to get back to work," Jennifer groaned, and then she added, "Please put Caroline's order on my tab."

"You don't have to do that," Caroline protested.

She felt her cheeks flush as she accepted Jennifer's offer. The cafe's prices were exorbitant, and even though Simon's coffee and treats were top-notch, they didn't warrant such costs.

"Nonsense," Jennifer insisted. "Consider it my treat. Besides, consider it a business expense, with you being my top client."

Simon turned to Caroline. "Can I get you your usual coffee while you peruse the menu?"

"Yes, please, Simon," Caroline replied with gratitude. Simon nodded and excused himself to fulfill their orders.

"I'd better get going," Jennifer said, her tone apologetic. "I'll see you back at my place this evening."

Caroline bid her friend farewell and Jennifer left the cafe, disappearing into the bustling city. As Caroline settled in, her coffee arrived, and she decided to forgo any food and instead set up her laptop. The cafe's creative ambiance was infectious, and she was eager to dive back into her writing.

With her laptop screen glowing before her, Caroline's thoughts drifted back over the past three years. Her father had passed away from a heart attack just two months before she'd discovered her husband, Robert Parker, was cheating on her. Two weeks after that revelation, she lost her job as the head of NYU Libraries.

Robert had insisted on keeping their house, a brownstone on the Upper West Side of New York, leaving Caroline and their twelve-year-old daughter, Jules, with nowhere to go. Jennifer had graciously taken them in, and they had lived in her three-bedroom Soho apartment for nearly six months, depleting Caroline's meager savings as she desperately searched for new employment.

However, there weren't many opportunities for a forty-four-year-old librarian in New York City. During Jules's school hours and between interviews, Caroline had begun writing "Cobble Cove Mysteries." Writing had become her refuge, a way to escape her shattered marriage, fading career, and the resentment of her now fourteen-year-old daughter.

Jules had been furious when Caroline uprooted their lives and moved them back to Plum Island, her small hometown in New England. She held Caroline responsible for the divorce and blamed her for everything that had gone wrong. However, their bond had recently started to mend as they collaborated on Caroline's new book, and the prospect of the TV series had brought them closer.

Caroline sighed contentedly and turned her attention back to her writing, eager to immerse herself in the world of her characters once more. However, her solitude was short-lived as a tall, impeccably dressed man approached her table. He appeared slightly flustered but politely asked if he could share her table.

Caroline surveyed the crowded cafe and realized that every seat was taken. She offered a friendly smile and gestured to the empty chair. "Of course, please have a seat."

The man smiled gratefully and settled into the chair across from her. He seemed like a creature from a different world, with his expensive attire and an air of sophistication that contrasted sharply with the cafe's casual atmosphere.

A server promptly arrived at their table, and the man ordered a sugary designer coffee concoction, which didn't take long to arrive.

Caroline couldn't help but suppress a shudder at the sweetness overload. The man seemed to notice her reaction and chuckled as he took a sip.

"I have a sweet tooth," he confessed, striking up a conversation. "My parents are always on my case about it. Even my sixteen-year-old son shakes his head at me when I have to satisfy my sugar cravings."

"My teenage daughter has a sweet tooth, too," Caroline mused.

"Really?" He chuckled. "Teenagers and their sweet tooth! It's a universal struggle, it seems." He held out his hand. "I'm Brad."

"Caroline." She shook his hand and noticed his handshake was firm but not rough.

As Caroline sipped her coffee, she soon found herself engaged in a pleasant conversation with Brad. While they chatted, Caroline couldn't help but observe him discreetly. Brad was a striking figure. She estimated his height to be roughly six foot three inches, just like her brother. His stylish, short, straight, jet-black hair was graced with subtle streaks of gray at the temples, framing a strong and handsome face that looked like a great artist chiseled it. Brad's piercing blue eyes sparkled with a warmth that drew you in, and when he smiled, it was nothing short of heart-stopping.

Their discussion meandered from favorite books to travel destinations, and Caroline found herself genuinely enjoying Brad's company.

It was a rarity for her to strike up conversations with strangers, especially a strange man. Caroline learned that he was from New York, but his job in the entertainment industry took him all over the world. He had a sixteen-year-old son, Connor, who was his pride and joy. The two of them had been close since his wife left them when Connor was eight months old. Except for a few visits, Connor didn't know his mother well, and he shied away from what he did know.

"I'm thankful that my son and I have such a close bond," Brad told her. "I always worried when I was younger that my kids wouldn't be as close to me as I was with my parents."

"Are your parents still around?" Caroline asked.

"Yes, my mother and father are still both fit and don't look a day older than fifty-five." Brad laughed. "Or so my mother likes to tell everyone."

"I was close to my parents, too," Caroline admitted.

"By was, you mean—" Brad's brows crinkled as he looked at her questioningly.

"My mother passed away ten years ago from cancer." Caroline swallowed the burning lump, thinking about her mother still brought to her throat. She cleared her throat. "My father passed away three years ago from a heart attack."

"I'm sorry." Brad's eyes filled with compassion. "Do you have siblings?"

"Yes, I have an older brother. He also lives in New England," Caroline told him. "Well, he's actually my half-brother. His mother passed away during childbirth."

"Oh, no, that's horrible," Brad said.

"My mother was a doctor at the hospital in Boston where my brother was born," Caroline explained. "His mother had a complicated pregnancy and had been hospitalized for her last two months."

"How did your parents end up getting together?" Brad's brows tightened in a curious frown.

"A year later, my father took my brother to the hospital because he was having breathing problems and was sent to a specialist at Boston General, where my mother worked." Caroline had no idea why she was blurting out her family history to a complete stranger, but Brad seemed genuinely interested. "They ran into each other again, and as my brother had to stay in hospital for tests for nearly two months, they saw each other daily." She smiled, thinking about the story her father told her. "One thing led to another, and they fell in love. My mother fell in love with the small town where my father lived and started a small practice on the island."

"You never wanted to become a doctor?" Brad frowned.

"Oh, no." Caroline's eyes widened. "I can't stand the sight of blood." She shuddered. "I was always more of a bookworm who loved to read. All I ever wanted to do was lose myself in stories."

"That's why you became a librarian." Brad smiled and sat back in the chair. "I'm glad libraries still exist with the internet being around."

"They do, but sadly, most of the books are being overlooked for the computers libraries have now." Caroline sighed. "I've just realized my life may seem such a bore compared to your jet-setting one."

"My life is tiring, and between you and me," Brad leaned forward and lowered his voice, "I'm actually afraid of flying."

"Oh, me too." Caroline nodded, wide-eyed. "I'm nervous while in the air, but I think the worst parts are the—"

"Take-off and landing," they said in unison and laughed.

"You know, I've always wanted to visit New England," Brad admitted. "The historic towns and the coastal beauty all sound incredibly charming."

"I can't believe you've been nearly everywhere there is to go in the United States, the world, and you've never been to New England." Caroline's eyes lit up as she spoke about her hometown. "It's a wonderful place. Although I spent most of my adult and married life in New York, my heart was still firmly planted in New England."

"Well, it's true," Brad assured her. "I've skirted around the area." He leaned back in his chair, a thoughtful expression on his face. "But hearing you talk about it and seeing how your eyes light up when you explain it, I'm definitely going to make an effort to get there."

Their conversation continued to flow effortlessly, touching on a myriad of topics. As the minutes turned into hours, Caroline found herself captivated by the man and surprised by the connection they were forming. It was a rare and unexpected pleasure, and she couldn't deny the sense of warmth that had enveloped her during their conversation.

The bustling coffee shop around them seemed to fade into the background as they shared stories and laughter. Time flew by, and Caroline couldn't help but feel a pang of disappointment when she realized how late it had gotten. She glanced at her wristwatch and then back at Brad.

"I should probably be heading back soon," Caroline said reluctantly. "The friend I'm staying with while I'm in New York will be waiting for me, and I have to check in with my daughter, who's staying with her father while we're in New York."

Brad nodded, a hint of regret in his eyes. "Of course. It's been a pleasure getting to know you."

Caroline gathered her things and stood up, and Brad stood with her. Her heart was heavy with the knowledge that she would have to say goodbye. But as she prepared to leave, Brad surprised her by extending an invitation.

"I know this is sudden, but would you like to join me for dinner tomorrow night?" Brad asked, his eyes filled with sincerity. "I'd love to continue our conversation."

Caroline hesitated for a moment, her mind racing. She barely knew Brad, and yet there was an undeniable connection between them. With a smile, she decided to take a leap of faith.

"I'd like that," she replied, her heart pounding with anticipation.

"Why don't we meet back here tomorrow evening around six?" Brad suggested.

"That sounds like a plan," Caroline said, hoping he couldn't hear how heavily her heart thudded against her rib cage. "Until tomorrow, then."

Brad raised her hand to his lips, gently kissing her knuckles. "Until tomorrow, Caroline."

Brad's smile was heart-stopping, and Caroline had to force her knees not to buckle under its impact. She gave herself a mental shake and gathered all her strength to walk out of the coffee shop without him seeing her jelly legs or collapsing in a puddle of mushy goo.

As she made her way to Jennifer's apartment, her mind was filled with images of Brad and how she'd had her first serendipitous moment. Caroline's footsteps echoed down the quiet corridor as she approached Jennifer's apartment. She couldn't shake the excitement from her chance encounter with him, the intriguing stranger who had entered her life so unexpectedly. Thoughts of their upcoming dinner date warmed her heart, and she couldn't wait to share the details with Jennifer.

As she reached Jennifer's door, Caroline fumbled for her keys, eager to get inside, but the door flew open before she could open it. Her anticipation turned to concern when she noticed Jennifer staring at her with an expression of a mixture of relief and worry.

"Caroline!" Jennifer exclaimed, her voice edged with worry as she grabbed Caroline and hugged her before pushing her away to look at her. "Where have you been? I've been trying to call you for ages. I was about to phone the police!"

Caroline checked her phone and was shocked to find a barrage of missed calls and messages from both Jennifer and Jules. She had been so engrossed in her conversation with Brad that she hadn't noticed her phone buzzing in her bag.

"I'm so sorry, Jen," Caroline apologized, feeling guilty for causing her friend so much distress. "I lost track of time. Let me check in with Jules. She's also been messaging."

Jennifer nodded, her concern easing. She stepped aside for Caroline to enter. Caroline dialed her daughter's number as she walked inside. Jules answered after the third ring. Before Caroline had finished greeting her daughter, she learned that Jules was upset because her father and his new wife were planning to convert her childhood bedroom into a nursery for their expected baby. Caroline did her best to placate her daughter, promising to talk to her father about finding a solution.

Once she hung up, Caroline hurriedly got ready, feeling a sense of urgency to make amends for her absence. Jennifer, who had been patient throughout, smiled as she saw Caroline's anxiousness.

"Don't worry," Jennifer reassured her. "We still have time to make our reservation at 'Le Petit Lueur.' It's one of the finest restaurants in Soho, and I'm sure you'll love it."

"I'm sure I will," Caroline said. "You know how much I love French cuisine."

Forty minutes later, they made their way to the restaurant. It was a hidden gem nestled in the heart of Soho. Its exterior was unassuming, but they were greeted by a warm, intimate atmosphere as they stepped inside. Soft candlelight flickered on white linen-covered tables, casting a romantic glow. The aroma of exquisite dishes filled the air, and the gentle hum of conversation added to the restaurant's charm.

Over a sumptuous meal, Caroline explained why she'd been so late returning to Jennifer's apartment. She shared the story of her chance meeting with Brad and how she'd agreed to go on a dinner date with him.

"Caroline, I can't believe you, of all people, agreed to go on a dinner date with a complete stranger!" Jennifer stared at her in disbelief.

"We spoke for hours," Caroline reminded her. "So, we're technically not strangers anymore."

"It is good to see you so perky and dreamy again." Jennifer smiled. "Maybe a New York fling will be good for you."

Caroline couldn't help but smile at her friend's openness to new possibilities. She agreed to download a tracking app on her phone, allowing Jennifer to keep an eye on her during the date, which put Jennifer's mind at ease.

As they finished their meal and took a leisurely stroll back to Jennifer's apartment, Jennifer finally revealed the reason behind her rushed meeting earlier in the day. Her voice carried a hint of sadness as she spoke.

"The truth is, the publishing house isn't doing well," Jennifer confessed. "They've decided to downsize, and I'm one of the people being laid off. In six months, I'll be unemployed."

Caroline's heart ached for her friend, knowing how much Jennifer had dedicated herself to her career in publishing. But she also saw an opportunity, a chance to inspire Jennifer to follow her own dreams as she'd done for Caroline.

Taking a deep breath, Caroline stopped walking and faced Jennifer. "Jen, I know this is a difficult time, but it might also be a chance for you to pursue what you've always wanted."

Jennifer looked puzzled, and Caroline continued, her voice filled with conviction.

"Remember how you've always wanted to open your own Entertainment Management firm? Publishing was supposed to be a stopgap until you could afford to do it. Maybe now is the time."

Jennifer's eyes widened as Caroline's words sank in. She had indeed dreamed of running her own company, guiding talent in the entertainment industry, and shaping careers. But life, with its demands and responsibilities, had pushed that dream aside.

Caroline placed a reassuring hand on Jennifer's shoulder. "Jennifer, this setback could be the universe's way of telling you it's time to follow your passion. It's never too late to chase your dreams, my friend."

She smiled. "Isn't that what you told me not too long ago? And look, I've got a book deal for my series and a television series."

Jennifer's face slowly lit up with hope and determination. "You know what? Maybe you're right. Perhaps it's time I took that leap of faith."

They continued their stroll. Caroline could see the weight of uncertainty lift from Jennifer's shoulders. As they walked together under the city's glittering skyline, Caroline couldn't help but feel that life had a way of weaving unexpected threads into their stories, leading them toward brighter tomorrows.

AVAILABLE TO ORDER SOON ON **AMAZON**

MORE BOOKS BY AMY RAFFERTY

SERIES

Christmas at Mistletoe Lodge ~ *A Feel Good Holiday Romance*

New Year at Mistletoe Lodge ~ *A Feel Good Holiday Romance*

Reunion at Mistletoe Lodge ~ *A Feel Good Holiday Romance*

The Bakery in Bar Harbor ~ *Secrets in Maine Series*

Cupids Bow Ranch ~ *Montana Country Inn Romance Series*

Starting Over in Nantucket ~ *Cody Bay Inn Series*

Leave a Rose in the Sand ~ *Starting Over in Key West Series*

A Mystery at Summer Lodge ~ *A Coastal Vineyard Series*

Charming Bookshop Mysteries ~ *Small Town Beach Romance*

Moonlight Dream ~ *Honey Bay Cafe Series*

Nantucket Christmas Escape ~ *Second Chance Holiday Ro-*
mance

Retreat ~ *Manatee Bay Series*

Secrets of White Sands Cove ~ *A San Diego Sunset Series*

The Seabreeze Cottage ~ *La Jolla Cove Series*

STANDALONE NOVELS

The McCaid Sisters ~ *A Second Chance Romance Mystery Novel*

BOX SETS

Montana Country Inn: The Complete Collection ~ *Montana Country Inn Romance Series*

Cody Bay Inn: The Complete Collection ~ *Nantucket Romance Series*

Starting Over in Key West: The Complete Collection ~ *A Florida Keys Romance Series*

A Mystery at Summer Lodge: The Complete Collection ~ *A Coastal Vineyard Series*

Charming Bookshop Mysteries: The Complete Collection ~ *Small Town Beach Romance*

Honey Bay Cafe Series: The Complete Collection ~ *Second Chance Beach Mystery Romance*

Nantucket Christmas Escape: The Complete Collection ~ *Second Chance Holiday Romance*

Manatee Bay: The Complete Collection ~ *Treasure Seekers Beach Romance Series*

Secrets of White Sands Cove: The Complete Collection ~ *A San Diego Sunset Series*

The Seabreeze Cottage: The Complete Collection ~ *La Jolla Cove Series*

THREE IN ONE

Coastal Collection: Sea Breeze Cottage, Mystery at Summer Lodge, Secrets of White Sands Cove ~ *Three Series in One Book*

SPANISH VERSION

El Café de Bahía Honey ~ *Honey Bay Cafe (Spanish)*

Escapada Navideña a Nantucket ~ *Nantucket Christmas Escape*
(Spanish)

Bahía de Manatee ~ *Manatee Bay (Spanish)*

La Posada de la Bahía Cody – *Cody Bay Inn (Spanish)*

AMY RAFFERTY VIP READERS

Subscribe Here!

Don't miss the Giveaways, competitions, and 'off the press' news!

Don't want to miss out on my giveaways, competitions,

and 'hot off the press' news?

Subscribe to my email list.

It is FREE!

Click Here!

CONNECT WITH AMY RAFFERTY

Not only can you check out the latest news and deals there, you can

also get

an email alert each time I release my next book.

Follow me on BookBub

I always love to hear from you and get your feedback.

Email me at ~ books@amyraffertyauthor.com

Follow on Amazon ~ Amy Rafferty

Sign up for my newsletter and free gift, Here

Join my 'Amy's Friends' group on Facebook

CONNECT WITH ROSE RYAN

Sign up for my newsletter and keep up on all the latest book news,

release dates,

excerpts, monthly giveaways, and more!

Or follow me on my other socials including:

Facebook , **Instagram**, **Bookbub** , and **Goodreads**

Follow my author central page on Amazon: **Rose Ryan:**

A NOTE FROM AMY RAFFERTY

Hi, wonderful people,

Having been described as "The Queen of Gorgeous Clean Mystery Romance," I am delighted that you are here.

I write sweet women's romance fiction for ages 20 and upwards. I bring you heartwarming, page-turning fiction featuring unforgettable families and friends and the ups and downs they face.

My mission is to bring you beach reads and feel-good fiction that fills your heart with emotion and love. You will find comfort in my strong female lead role models, along with the men who love them. Fill your hearts with family saga, the power of friendship, second chances, and later-in-life romance.

I write books you cannot put down, bringing sunshine to your days and nights.

Thank you for being here and reading my books x

A NOTE FROM ROSE RYAN

Hi, incredible people,

I love writing women's romance novels that are sweet, filled with mystery plots, heartfelt emotions, family drama and second chances.

I welcome you to join me on this exciting adventure of writing heart-warming contemporary beach romance novels.

Also, it would mean the world to me if you would kindly leave a review on my stories using the link below which takes you to my author page on Amazon.

I appreciate you all.

I hope my writing brings happiness and inspiration to you!

Thanks for being here!

Rose x

Made in the USA
Monee, IL
18 March 2024